BLACK CONTRACT

CHARLOTTE BYRD

GW00569978

CONTENTS

"FAST-PACED, DARK, ADDICTIVE, AND COMPELLING" -
Clpetit56, amazon reviewer

"HOT, STEAMY, AND A GREAT STORYLINE." - Christine
Reese

"MY OH MY....CHARLOTTE has made me a fan for life."
- JJ, amazon reviewer

"THE TENSION and chemistry is at five alarm level." -
Sharon, amazon reviewer

"HOT, sexy, intriguing journey of Elli and Mr. Aiden
Black. - Robin Langelier

"GREAT START TO FANTASTIC SERIES!" - Brenda,
amazon reviewer

"SEXY, STEAMY AND CAPTIVATING!" - Charmaine,
amazon reviewer

" INTRIGUE, lust, and great characters...what more could you ask for?!" - Dragonfly Lady

"AN AWESOME BOOK. Extremely entertaining, captivating and interesting sexy read. I could not put it down." - Kim F, amazon reviewer

"JUST THE ABSOLUTE BEST STORY. Everything I like to read about and more. Such a great story I will read again and again. A keeper!!" - Wendy Ballard

"THIS SERIES THRILLED me from the first page and had me completely engrossed.

The pacing and plot was excellent. It had the perfect amount of twists and turns, luring me into the fantasy of this amazing book.

The story was well-crafted, starting off with characters I fell in love with. I instantaneously bonded with the heroine and of course Mr. Black. YUM.

It's sexy, it's sassy, it's steamy. It's everything.

I loved every second of it and was so thrilled to have had such a treat." - Khardine Gray, bestselling romance author

ABOUT BLACK CONTRACT

T*hey can take everything from me, but they can't take her.*

Mr. Black is coming back. With a vengeance.

"I need you to sign a contract."

"What kind of contract?"

"A contract that will make you mine."

This time she's going to do everything I say.

She's going to hate it and then she's going to beg for more.

This is the game we play. It's our game.

But what happens when others find out? Will we lose everything?

CHAPTER 1 - ELLIE

I don't want to look at my phone. I want to be mad at him. I don't want to hear what he has to say.

But I can't stop myself.

The texts just keep coming in. I can't resist.

I know what he's going to say. Yet, I have to see it myself.

In print.

I'm really sorry.

I need to talk to you.

Please.

I refuse to reply, but my phone keeps going off.

I know you're not asleep yet because your light is on.

Can I please come up?

MY HEART SKIPS A BEAT. He's downstairs. Shit. The feeling that surges through my body is hard to explain. It's some combination of dread and excitement. What is he doing here? Why isn't he still with that blonde? A hundred other questions rush through my mind as I try to decide what to do.

No. I'm going to bed, I text back.

ELLIE, please. I have to talk to you. I need you.

I NEED YOU. What does that mean? I wonder. I'm tempted to say no again, but I know that I won't be able to sleep a wink if I do.

YOU HAVE FIVE MINUTES, I text and climb out of bed.

I walk down the cold parquet floor barefoot, regretting the fact that I didn't put on a pair of socks.

When I buzz him in, I unlock the front door and head back to my room to look for a pair of slippers.

"Hey," Aiden whispers, startling me. He's leaning on the doorframe to my room, looking as handsome and brooding as ever.

"How did you get here so fast?" I ask as he tries to catch his breath.

"The elevator was taking too long so I ran up the stairs."

"Four floors?"

He shrugs. "It probably would've been faster to just go wait, but I couldn't keep my legs still."

I smile at the thought of this.

"Listen, Ellie, the reason I wanted to come up is to tell you..." his voice drops off. I wait for him to continue, but he doesn't.

"Yes?"

"Just seeing you again at the club…it just made me realize what a horrible mistake I made."

"What do you mean?" I ask.

"It was so stupid of me to break our engagement. I hate to say that I didn't mean it, but I actually didn't. I was just going through a lot with getting fired and then that article came out. I wasn't thinking. I was totally lost."

I nod and look away. I understand and sympathize with what he was going through, but that doesn't change all the hurt that he caused me.

"It's okay, I guess," I say after a moment. It's definitely not okay, but there isn't much to say in situations like these, is there?

"No, it's not. I was an asshole. And I was wrong. And I'm here to apologize to you. I know that you probably can't forgive me immediately, but I just need you to know that."

I nod.

"There's something else, too."

I wait for him to elaborate.

"Do you think there's any chance that you could take me back?" he asks, taking a step toward me.

"What?" I take a step back.

"I love you, Ellie. I should have never said any of those things. I didn't mean a word of it. I want you back, Ellie."

Tears of frustration and anger start to well up somewhere in the back of my throat, but I refuse to let him see them. I swallow hard and clench my fists.

"What are you doing, Aiden?"

"What do you mean?"

"You think I'm an idiot? A fool or something?"

"No, not at all!"

"Yes, you do," I say. "We don't know each other well, but I never thought that you were this cruel and heartless."

"What are you talking about?" Aiden shakes his head.

"I saw you!" My voice breaks a little. He stares at me, dumbfounded.

"You need to leave," I say after a moment. "If you refuse to admit it then I just can't deal with it. You're not the person I thought you were."

"Ellie, seriously, I have no idea what you're talking about."

I stare at him. How can he just lie to me like this? So effortlessly. Maybe I didn't know him as well as I thought I did.

"I need you to leave," I say after a moment.

"Ellie, please. Can you just tell me what you're talking about?"

I finally lose it. "I'm talking about tonight. I saw you with that blonde with the long legs. She was all over you."

"What?" Aiden asks with a perplexed look on his face. "Oh, Annie? You mean the girl I walked into the club with?"

I nod and cross my arms across my chest. I don't have time for this charade.

"That's Annie. She's my friend, John's, fiancée. I've known her for years."

This is not the direction that I had expected this conversation to go.

"Why was she all over you like that?"

"She wasn't. I was really upset tonight. It was their idea to take me out. She was just hugging me to make me feel better. John was right there."

I still don't fully believe him, but I also know that Aiden is either telling the truth or the biggest sociopath ever.

"Listen, I can tell that you don't believe me. Let me show you," he says, taking out his phone. He flips to Facebook and shows me pictures of Annie and John, the happy couple since high school. I didn't see John there, but that was definitely Annie who had her arm around Aiden.

"If you want, I can call them right now. Or just call John and ask them where we were tonight."

I don't really want him to do that because I know it will make me look like the most insecure girl ever, and yet I do. When I don't reply right away, Aiden dials John's number. Without really explaining why, he tells him that he's on speakerphone and asks him where he and Annie were today.

"Um, are you okay, Aiden?"

"Yes. Just please answer, okay."

"Okay...we were with you, at the club in Chelsea. That is until you ran out on us."

"Yeah, why did you do that, Aiden?" Annie pipes in. "You know we were only going there to cheer you up. It's not exactly our scene."

After joking around for a few minutes, Aiden hangs up the phone and looks at me.

"Okay, I guess she is who you say she is," I say.

"I would never lie to you, Ellie. Maybe I should've back then after dinner with your parents, but I couldn't lie to you then either. I love you."

CHAPTER 2- ELLIE

WHEN HE SLEEPS OVER…

I'm not one for quick decision making, especially when my mind is still in somewhat of a fog. After talking to Aiden for close to an hour about where he stands and where I stand, I'm no closer to getting any sort of clarity about any of this. What I do get though, is a throbbing headache.

"Let me get you some Advil," Aiden says. "It's getting late, then you need to rest."

He's right, of course. But I can't help wondering whether my need to rest also comes with his need to leave. Frankly, that's the last thing I want.

Aiden comes back from the kitchen with a glass of

water and a bottle of headache medicine. I swallow a few tablets and sit down on my bed.

"Can I ask you something? But you have to promise not to take it the wrong way."

"Okay," he says quietly, bracing himself for the worst.

"Would you mind spending the night?"

"What?" his eyes light up.

"Just as friend for now. I can't think about all of the rest of that stuff right now."

I expect the expression on his face to fall, but much to my surprise, it doesn't. His eyes continue to shine with brilliance.

"Yes, of course. I'd love to," he whispers. "Why don't you get in bed and I'll just make myself comfortable right here."

"On the chair?" I ask.

"Yep."

"No, no, no. You can't sleep on the chair," I say. "That

chair is awful. I get a backache just from sitting in it for an hour. Just come and sleep in bed with me, okay? Friends do that you know."

"Really?" Aiden asks. "I've never heard of friends sleeping together in the same bed except maybe on *Dawson's Creek*."

"Now, that's a blast from the past," I say, pulling back the covers.

I SLEEP IN LATE. It's after ten when I finally open my eyes. Even though I've been getting a lot of sleep over the last few days, this is the first time that I actually wake up rested.

"Oh hey," I say, sitting up in bed and stretching. "What are you doing here?"

"You asked me to spend the night," Aiden says. He's sitting in the chair in the corner of the room, reading a book.

"Are you reading Danielle Steel?" I ask.

"I've never read her before. She's actually quite good."

"Well, yeah, she did sell like six-hundred and fifty million books."

"Is that true?"

I nod. I actually looked it up recently. I've never read her stuff until a month ago either, and since then I raced through four books, unable to put them down.

Aiden puts the book on the nearby table and walks over to me.

"You look beautiful," Aiden says, sitting down on the bed. I look away, slightly embarrassed at his comment. I haven't even brushed my teeth or washed my face, let alone put on some makeup.

Suddenly, he reaches out and brushes his fingers along my bottom lip. He leans closer to me. His fingertips feel rough and effervescent at the same time. I close my eyes and lick my lips as I feel the softness of his breath on my cheek. Slowly, Aiden cradles my face and buries his fingers in my hair. I close my eyes and press my lips against his.

His lips are as soft as I remember, I can almost taste the kindness through them. He tilts my head back, dropping his. Slowly, he runs his lips up my neck. Shivers run up my spine in exhilaration. When he takes my shoulders in his hands, our legs touch and I feel his body against mine. He's pressing against me, and my legs open up on their own. Within a few moments, our bodies intertwine and we become one.

"Wait," I whisper.

Aiden pulls away, reluctantly and waits. I don't really have anything else to say except that this feels... strange. Not really wrong, but not really entirely right either. I look up at him. His face is so close to mine that when his hair falls into his face, it brushes against mine as well.

"What's wrong?" Aiden asks.

I shrug, and look away. He takes a step closer, even though it hardly feels as if there's any room for a step to take between us.

"Nothing. I don't know."

He moves his face closer to mine, but does not kiss me. Instead, he closes and opens his eyes and lets me feel the softness of his eyelashes on my cheek. These butterfly kisses make my knees grow weak.

"I want you," he whispers, without moving a muscle. He wants me to make the next move. And suddenly, I can't think of a reason not to. Whatever reasons I had to push him away are no longer relevant. I'd give anything to be in the warm embrace of his strong arms again. We belong together.

"I want you too," I say.

"Show me," he says, smiling with his whole face. His piercing eyes twinkle in the morning light.

I take him by the hand and lead him back to bed. I lay down first and pull him on top of me. He lowers himself slowly. When he settles on top of me, his smile disappears, and yet his face keeps that familiar whimsical and mysterious expression.

"You're beautiful," I whisper. "You're the most beautiful man I've ever seen in my whole life."

He smiles again. I've never been that open with anyone before, not even with Aiden himself.

"I love you," he whispers. My cheeks flush red. How, after everything that we've been through, he can still make me blush is difficult to comprehend. He kisses me again, this time more forcefully. Pressing his whole body into mine, he overwhelms me with his strength. I love how hard his body feels on top of me, taking mine as his. I kiss him back, with just as much force. As I push back into him, I feel him rise a little above me.

Quickly, our bodies begin to move as one. We are no longer tepid or unfamiliar with what each of us desires. Through his pants, I feel the largeness of his hard cock and I can't wait to see it again. I need to feel it in my bare hand. I need to taste it.

Aiden's hand slides down my body, making its way under my shirt and underneath my pajama pants. His lips pull away from mine and make their way down to my belly button. When he kisses my hip bones, my hips move up and down involuntarily.

Aiden pulls off my pajama pants and then helps me out of my shirt. He swiftly takes off his own pants and shirt and settles back on top of me. He licks my belly button and then runs his tongue along the top of my panties. With each kiss, my body rises and falls and I close my legs to stop myself from getting wet. But it's too late for that.

Seeing my legs closing access, Aiden pushes them open and buries his face within them. My mouth immediately dries up, sucking all moisture within my body and concentrating it between my legs. I throw my head back in pleasure and run my hands over my rock hard nipples.

"I've missed you," Aiden says, running his tongue around my clit in small concentric circles that make me want to scream. I bury my hands in his hair and pull until he moans.

I've missed him. I've wanted him for so long and now that he's mine, I can't keep my pleasure at bay. A few moments later, Aiden pulls away from me and I reach down to grab his cock.

"I want you," he says, taking my nipple in between his teeth.

"I want you too," I mumble.

Unable to keep my body from salivating further, I push him deep within me. I relish in the surprise look on his face for a moment, until the pleasure of him being within me overwhelms me completely. My legs get that all too familiar cramping feeling, before going numb and a warm sensation starts to fill my body from my core out to every extremity.

"I love you," I whisper as my body gets closer and closer to that blissful release.

"I love you, too," Aiden moans in my ear. He pushes himself in and out of me faster and faster until we both collapse into each other's arms a few moments later. A simultaneous orgasm. I've never had one before and I close my eyes to keep the room from spinning around me.

WE LAY in each other's arms in total bliss for close to an hour without really saying much. It's nice to just be with someone without feeling the need to talk to fill dead air.

"I love you, Ellie," Aiden says after a while.

"I love you too."

"I just wanted to tell you that when I wasn't inside of you."

"Thanks? I guess. I don't really know how to respond to that," I laugh.

"No, what I mean is that I didn't want you to think that I only said that because I was overwhelmed by pleasure. I mean, I was, but I love you for real, whether or not we're having sex."

I laugh.

"Okay, that came out quite awkward as well. You'll have to forgive me. I've had a very emotional twenty-four hours."

Wow, has it only been twenty-four hours? I wonder to myself.

"Okay, so, I've been thinking about something," Aiden says. "I don't know where you stand on the whole engagement thing anymore, and I don't want to pressure you in any way. But I have another proposal for you."

"Another proposal?"

"Yes. Now that I'm a properly unemployed bum—"

"With millions of dollars," I interrupt jokingly.

"You're right. Now that I'm a properly unemployed bum with millions of dollars, I was wondering if you would be interested in taking a trip with me. I'm thinking of taking my yacht and sailing it down to the Caribbean."

I sit up and look at him.

"For how long?"

"I don't know," he shrugs. "A couple of weeks. A couple of months. Forever?"

I inhale deeply and consider the proposition.

"C'mon, imagine all those turquoise waters, palm trees swaying in the gentle breeze, eight-five degree weather, swimming with manatees? How can you say no to that?"

I think about it for a moment. That does sound like an amazing experience.

"What about your work?" I ask.

"What work?"

"I don't know. But weren't you going to try to figure out what you were going to do next?"

"Yes. And what better place than on some white sandy beach holding a drink with a little straw hat?"

I nod. He has a good point there.

"And you can always write there as well. Or on the yacht. I have a number of rooms, which you can use as your office."

"And this would be for an indefinite period of time?" I ask.

"For as long as or as little as you want."

"So, what you're basically asking me, Aiden Black, is whether or not I want to move in with you on your yacht?" I ask, jokingly.

"Yes, I guess I am. What do you say?"

Who doesn't love the idea of sailing away to some exotic place, far away from all of their problems? I'm no exception. I take one last moment to try to think of a reason to say no, but nothing comes to me.

"Okay, why not?" I finally say.

Aiden throws his arms around me and pushes me back down on the bed.

"You have made me very happy Ellie Rhodes," he whispers in my ear in between his kisses. "I just hope you give me the chance to do the same for you."

You already have, I think to myself and kiss him back.

CHAPTER 3 - ELLIE

The idea of going to the Caribbean isn't anything that is well-planned. But I've had a lot of planning for a while. It's just something that he proposed we do and the next thing I know, we're taking off.

"So, you're leaving? Just like that?" Caroline asks. I nod as I pack my bag. I don't really know what to bring. All of my summer clothes are packed away in the back of my closet and I'm struggling to get them out.

Caroline is pretty much up to date on everything that has been going on. Our failed engagement. The Page Six article that revealed me as a romance

writer, and the yacht auction where I met and
started dating Aiden Black. His firing as CEO of Owl.

"I promise that I will be back soon," I say. We still
haven't talked much about what happened to her in
Maine. All I know is that Tom was arrested and
charged with rape and assault and he's awaiting trial.
She will be the star witness against him. I am also
expected to testify, since he attacked me as well. But
I haven't heard anything from the District Attorney,
or her attorney, about any of this.

"I'm going to have my cell phone with me. And I will
have email as well. That way, if anything happens
with the case, I will be available. I'll take the first
flight out."

Caroline looks away. She hates talking about this,
but we have to. I need her to know that I'm going to
be there for her, no matter what.

"This whole thing...it's just a bit much to deal with,"
Caroline says. Suddenly, something occurs to me.
Perhaps she wants me to stay. Maybe she needs me
more than I thought she did.

"Do you want me to cancel the trip?" I ask.

Caroline shakes her head. "Don't be silly."

"It's not silly. It's no problem. I mean, I'll stay if you want me to."

Caroline just shrugs her shoulders and looks away. "I'm going to be fine. I'm just worrying about this for nothing. The trial isn't for another month probably, who the hell knows. You should go and have fun."

"And what are you going to do?" I ask.

"Talk to my therapist. Go to work."

I'm glad that she has started to see someone about this. I've been asking her to go for some time, but she kept resisting.

"Go out maybe?" I ask. I know Caroline won't be back to being her old self unless she starts to go out again and have fun.

"Yeah, maybe." She shrugs. Okay, maybe that was wishful thinking. For now, I should be happy that she's just going out to work and to the therapist.

"Is the shrink helping?" I ask. When she went to her first session, she refused to talk about it except to say that it went fine. I'm hoping to get a little bit more info about it now that some time has passed.

"She said it's going to be an uphill climb to get over it, but it's going to be okay in the end."

I nod.

"I just don't think I have the energy, Ellie. I just feel so tired all the time."

I nod and put my arm around her.

"I'm really, really sorry, Ellie. I just wish there were something I could do."

"You can."

"What?"

"I want you to testify against him. No matter what."

"Yes, of course, I will. Caroline, just because I'm going on this trip doesn't mean that I'm not going to testify. The minute that your lawyer or the DA need me, I'm there."

"Okay, that's good," Caroline says, wiping the outside of her eye. Is she crying? Why would she think that I wouldn't testify on her behalf? My mind spins a mile a minute.

"I love you," I say and wrap my arms around her.

"I love you, too."

I finish packing the rest of the time alone. Caroline says that she's tired and goes to her room to lie down. She just woke up an hour ago, but she doesn't have much energy these days. I again deliberate whether it's such a good idea for me to leave her alone at this point. But when I voice my concerns out loud, she says that she's planning on going to visit her family for a few days. So, there's no need for me to hang around anyway. No one will be here.

With great effort, I manage to retrieve my large box of summer clothes from the back of my closet, I look through the contents and pick out a few tank tops and shorts that I think will work well in the Caribbean. I also try on every swimsuit I own and I'm disappointed to find that they, unfortunately, do not fit as well as they did last summer. Damn the sugar and carbs that were too hard to resist in the long dark days without Aiden. I decide to not give them any more thought and just toss them into my suitcase. I'm not going to let the fact that I look (or maybe just feel) fat prevent me from taking the trip of a lifetime with the man of my dreams.

Speaking of which, I still don't exactly know where the hell we are really headed. When I agreed to go, I said yes to the Caribbean. But the Caribbean has hundreds of islands and at least half a dozen different countries. The precise location of where we are headed is still unknown.

WHERE EXACTLY ARE WE HEADED? I text Aiden.

The Caribbean, he texts back.

Yes, but where?

It's a surprise. I'll pick you up at seven.

I SMILE and return to my suitcase. At first, I was thinking that a carry-on would be enough, but after going back and forth between all of my blouses and different dresses and finally deciding to take them all, nothing but a large suitcase that weighs over fifty pounds will do.

Aiden picks me up on time. This time, we have a driver who helps me with my bag. Aiden just stands near the car and takes me into his arms.

"You're not going to need this," he whispers, petting my thick winter coat with his hands.

"Well, it's freezing out here and I didn't want to be cold when we came back."

"And what if we don't?"

"Ever come back?"

"Yep." He presses his lips onto mine. "What if we decide to just stay and live on the yacht? Maybe go all the way across the Atlantic and then around the world."

I consider that for a moment. "That does sound...nice."

"Let's do it then," he says, kissing my hand. I smile at him. "Let's just see how it goes at first."

I'm not sure why I'm hesitating. I don't really have anything to come back to here. My relationship with my mom and Mitch is a bit on the rocks and I don't really have the strength to try to make it any better. I can write and publish from anywhere. The only thing that I do have is Caroline. I hate to admit it, but one of the main reasons I want to go on this trip is to get away from her. I hate how helpless I feel around her. I want to do something to make her better, but everything I do is futile. Nothing seems to help one bit.

"I need to come back for Caroline's trial."

"Yes, of course." Aiden nods. The expression on his face immediately turns sour.

"You might need to testify, too."

"Of course."

We ride in silence for a while.

"How is she?" he asks.

"I don't really know. She doesn't talk much. She seems better, but she might be just pretending. I have no idea."

Caroline isn't much of a pretender. She's a sharer - an over-sharer. This is the girl who told me every sordid detail about her sex life without batting an eye. And yet, I have no idea how she's really coping with what happened in Maine. Or with the upcoming trial.

"She said she's going to visit her family while I'm away."

"That's good."

Caroline doesn't have the best relationship with her family. Her mom is quite self-centered and I doubt that she would be much help in this type of situation. Still, I'm glad that she's getting out of the house and doing something.

"I sort of feel guilty leaving her."

"I'm sorry. I guess you can invite her along,"
Aiden says.

I look over at him. "Really?"

He nods.

"I never considered that."

"Well, consider it now."

Inviting Caroline will make this whole situation
much less of a fun trip. I mean, if she was the old
Caroline, maybe I would consider it.

"What?" Aiden asks.

"I'm just touched by your offer." I pick up his hand
and kiss it. "I mean, you don't have to invite her and I
really appreciate it."

"Listen, I know that she has been through a lot.
And none of what she went through is fair. Tom is
a huge asshole and I can't wait to see him get
convicted in court for everything that he has done.
And I know that she's your best friend, so
why not?"

I pat Aiden on the knee. "I don't think she will be
into it," I say after a moment. "Besides, I'm not sure

that you really know what you're offering at
this point."

"Oh, yeah?"

"Yeah. Caroline is fun, but not this version of
Caroline. Now, she's mopey and depressed and not
someone who you want accompanying you on a
sexcapade."

"Sexcapade?" Aiden asks. "Did I hear you correctly?
Is that what you're doing?"

"I figure." I shrug and flash him a coy smile. "I think
we're due for some fun. And what better place than
your yacht, right?"

THE TOWN CAR drops us off at a private airport where
two large men who look like really high-end
bodyguards help us with our bags. I walk up the
open-air stairs toward the door of a luxurious
airplane, the likes of which I've only seen in movies.

"Is this yours?"

"Not anymore, unfortunately. Now, it's just a rental."

Hmm, a rental? I had no idea that private airplanes could be rented. I enter the cabin and my mouth drops open. The seats are wide and spacious and fold all the way back like they do in very upscale movie theaters. The floors are hardwood and there's enough space in the place to do cartwheels.

"This plane is amazing," I whisper in awe.

"Yes, it's a bit different than flying coach, isn't it?"

A flight attendant, who introduces herself as Alexa, asks us what we would like to drink.

"I'm not sure," I say shyly. I'm sort of craving some alcohol to really kick off this trip, but I'm not sure if they have any available.

"I'd like an old-fashioned, please," Aiden says. Alexa has long toned legs and breasts which are natural and to die for, but he barely blinks an eye. "Ellie? You want a cocktail?"

"Yes...a mojito please."

Alexa comes back in a few minutes with both of our drinks. Taking a sip of mine, I lose myself in the moment as the refreshing mint mixed with rum runs down the back of my throat.

"This is delicious," I say.

A few moments later, we take off. The ascent is so smooth, I barely notice a thing until my ears pop. Instead, I drink more of my mojito and stare into Aiden's piercing eyes.

"So, are you going to tell me where we are headed?" I ask once we are cruising at thirty-thousand feet.

"Nope," Aiden says with a wide smile across his face.

"Really?"

"Really. All you have to know is that we're headed where my yacht is waiting for us."

A FEW HOURS LATER, we land at a private airport in the middle of the night and take a helicopter to his yacht. Someone from the staff takes our bags to his stateroom while Aiden invites me out onto the top deck to look at the stars. I lean into his shoulder and look up. We stand here, looking up at the sparkling sky and the bright yellow moon above without saying a word.

I listen to Aiden inhale and exhale deeply and smile. He looks down at me with admiration. I close my eyes and enjoy the gaze that washes over me. I want to stay in this moment forever. Somewhere in the distance, I hear the soothing voice of Adele belting out another song about heartbreak.

I look up at him. I admire his chiseled jaw and his luscious lips. He exhales deeply, bringing me closer. Another inhale and I'm his. He pulls me toward him and presses his lips to mine. His tongue brushes against the inside of my lower lip. My hands move up his neck and bury themselves in his thick luscious hair. When I tug a little, he moans in pleasure.

His hand presses on the small of my back and I sense that familiar hardness through his immaculate gray suit. I pull his body against mine and let him hold me as if he has no intention of ever letting me go.

A cool breeze comes off the ocean, swirling around us. We are standing perfectly still, but I suddenly feel as if I'm falling. No, it's as if I have jumped. From a very great height. I'm falling and the ground is getting closer and closer, and the only thing that can stop me from colliding with it is him. His love. This feeling of exhilaration consumes me.

Aiden whispers my name, sending shivers up my spine. There's a longing in his voice. I feel him wanting me. Craving me. As much as I want him. Perhaps no one has ever wanted me more than he does right now.

When I look up at him, I'm faced with a familiar expression of darkness mixed with light.

CHAPTER 5 - AIDEN

I watch Ellie walk into the stateroom, leaving me alone on the deck.

She said yes. Yes. Not to the engagement quite yet. I really fucked that up, but to the trip to Caribbean. I close my eyes and imagine her naked before me. I want to touch her everywhere. I want to do bad things to her. I want her to scream my name at the top of her lungs.

My phone rings. I look down and immediately regret not turning it off. I shouldn't answer it, of course. I know that already. But I can't really stop myself. It's one of my many attorneys. Neil Goss. He's going to bill me for this phone call as if it were in person, as if we had met at his office, or had lunch at a rate of

$500 per hour. There are no discounts for the fact
that he doesn't have to get off his butt or even be at
his desk. He even bills me for the time he spends
waiting for the phone to ring and leave a message. I
know. I've seen one of his bills recently. But I guess I
should be thankful for the fact that I'm not also
paying for his food and drinks. You see, after I was
fired from my job as CEO of Owl, the startup I
started, that grew to be the main competitor to
Amazon, I have to pay for all of my legal fees myself.
Frankly, I'm not even sure if this guy is worth the
money, but I can't really fire him because my
situation is quite complicated and I'd have to spend
a lot of time explaining to another - new - attorney.
Along with all the paperwork that he would
inevitably have to read through and analyze, it
would cost me at least forty hours of time. At the end
of the day, this guy isn't that bad. I mean, how
different are lawyers anyway, right?

"Hello?"

"Aiden, I have some news."

What I do appreciate about Neil is that because he
charges me for every minute of talking, he doesn't
waste a second of it on small talk. I doubt he's much

of a small talk person anyway, but it is a little bit of a perk.

"What is it?"

"The board isn't happy with the new CEO. The company isn't doing well."

"You mean Blake?"

After the Board of Directors fired me, they set up my old friend Blake Garrison as the interim CEO before they got a chance to go through a full list of qualified candidates. On paper, Blake is, of course, as qualified as I am. He has an Ivy League education. Many years at the company working in various upper management positions. He was the guy who brought us all of the original investors. And of course, he's also the guy who then, conveniently, got rid of those investors after assaulting Ellie on this very yacht. What an asshole.

"Are they getting rid of him?"

"That's what they're saying through the grapevine." The rumors that Neil has access to are usually spot on. He's the one who first told me that they were thinking of firing me. It gave me a day to prepare for the inevitable and not make a fool out of myself in the boardroom.

"I don't know if you've checked recently, but the stock price is plummeting. From what I hear, the Board thought that getting rid of you would renew confidence in the company, but clearly it hasn't. So, they're thinking of getting rid of Blake."

Whoever Neil has on the inside has access to some deep undercover shit.

"This isn't exactly bad news," I point out.

"They aren't decided yet. They're having an emergency meeting soon and putting it out to a vote. We'll just have to see what happens."

I nod. "I'm glad that they're considering getting rid of him, but without a solid replacement, it will just make the company seem even more unstable."

"Unfortunately, I have to agree with you."

Both Neil, as well as many of the attorneys who work for him, and I are heavily invested in Owl. Even though I got ousted, most of my severance package is tied to Owl's stock price. So, the fact that it's plummeting isn't exactly music to my ears.

"They wouldn't just replace him with someone else who is not very well known, would they?" I ask. At this point, Owl needs a savior. Someone with vision and ideas. Someone who gets where the company is going and how to help it get there in the most efficient way possible. Someone like me.

"I hope not," Neil says. He hangs up soon after, saying that he has to get back to work. This is either true or he's just trying to save me a few bucks. Either way, I'm grateful because with the stock price dropping like a rock and all of my other money being tied up in big real estate projects around town, I need to start being careful with money again.

I look out at the dark ocean and lose myself in the past. It wasn't too long ago that I was a big shot CEO of one of the fastest growing startups around. But it wasn't just my job that I loved. It was what I had built, created, with my own hands. Back in college, Owl was just an idea. More like a kernel of an idea. I had an idea for a website where people bought and sold things, pretty much like eBay and Amazon but slightly different. Everything would be cheaper and the shipping would take a bit longer. I believed that despite everyone's interest in getting things as soon as possible, they also wanted to save money. And the way that they could save a few bucks, or a lot of bucks, is to simply wait a bit longer for the shipping.

Well, as time passed and we started this site with just a few items and no listing fees, it slowly grew into a bigger and bigger marketplace. The first wave of investors helped to make it what it is now, a publicly traded company on the New York Stock Exchange. But the next wave? Well, before they fired me, I was in the middle of investing heavily into advertising. Everyone hates ads, but everyone loves them as well. When ads are targeted properly, you love them because they expose you to products that are perfect just for you. And with the right algorithm, I knew that I could properly match consumers with their ideal sellers and products. Of course, to develop this area, we needed more investment. Blake was in the process of doing that again, until he fucked me. Well, what goes around comes around, right? I had laid out my whole strategy for moving this company over to the next level. All he had to do was follow it. But, of course, he couldn't. His ego wouldn't let him follow any of my blueprints. As much as I want to see him fail, I don't want his failure to fuck up everything that I have worked so hard for my whole adult life. So, I find his downfall kind of bittersweet. He's going down and he's taking Owl with him.

Ellie comes outside and approaches me. She wraps her arms around me and gives me a big squeeze.

"This is beautiful," she whispers, looking up at me. "It's even more beautiful when it's just the two of us."

This yacht is huge for just two people. Well, not just two people, there is the staff. But just two guests.

"It's quite different than from the last time you were here, isn't it?" I ask. She nods and puts her head on my shoulder. I lean my head toward hers as well. We stare up at the stars together.

"You're the most beautiful woman in the world."

Ellie looks up at me and shakes her head.

"You don't believe me?"

She shrugs her shoulder in that shy way that makes her even more attractive.

"I'm going to do bad things to you," I say after a moment. As much as I love her right now, I always crave her. This trip to the Caribbean is going to be so much more than a trip for us to get to know each other. No, I need to blow off some steam. Way too much shit has happened recently to both of us. And we deserve some time to...get to know each other in another way.

"Oh, really?" she asks, her eyes twinkling in the starlight. "Like what?"

"Mr. Black is coming back. With a vengeance."

Her body quivers, but she doesn't budge.

I inhale deeply. This is something I've been thinking about for quite some time. But other things have come up, gotten in the way. And now, well, the timing couldn't be better.

"I need you to sign a contract."

"What kind of contract?"

"A contract that will make you mine for the duration of this trip."

She looks surprised, appalled even. But then a small smile forms at the corner of her lips.

CHAPTER 6 - ELLIE

WHEN HE EXPLAINS THE CONTRACT...

A contract? What kind of contract? I have a million questions and my heart starts to pound a million miles a minute. The wind comes off the ocean. My whole body starts to shiver, but I'm entirely sure that it has nothing to do with the balmy Caribbean air. No, this is something else. Anxiety, mixed with anticipation and excitement.

"What are you talking about, Mr. Black?" I ask. He hasn't been Mr. Black for a while. I won't lie, it's nice to have him back. These past few months have been filled with so much complicated shit that it's nice to step away from reality for a moment. Or evening. Or a few days.

"I want you to sign a contract to be mine for the duration of this trip," Aiden says. His voice is lower now. More stern. He's starting to embody Mr. Black.

"And what would that entail?"

"You would do everything that I tell you to do when I tell you to do it," he says. His eyes are laser-focused on mine.

"Everything?" I ask.

"Everything."

At first, I'm not sure how to respond. But after a moment, I flash him a smile. He takes my arm in his and pulls me to his stateroom. My heart skips a few beats as I follow him.

I SIT DOWN on the edge of his large, California king bed and he walks over to the large oak desk in the corner. A few moments later, he hands me a contract.

I will agree to any sexual activity deemed fit by Mr. Black except those previously negotiated.

I will agree to wear whatever clothing deemed fit by Mr. Black.

I will accompany Mr. Black wherever he wishes to go.

I agree to follow these terms for the following duration: _____.

THERE IS a place for me to initial at every line and sign at the bottom. My head spins for a moment.

"WHAT IS THIS?" I ask.

"The contract. Something for us to experiment with while we are on this trip."

"I thought we would just have fun," I say.

"Yes, we will."

"So, why do we need this?"

"To make it more official."

Honestly, I have no idea how I feel about this. Make things more official? I already postponed the engagement.

"This doesn't feel right, Aiden," I say after a moment. He looks disappointed.

"What don't you like about it?"

"Well, I'm not entirely sure what sexual activities I'm agreeing to and which ones I'm rejecting."

"Ah, yes." He smiles. "Here's the second page with hard limits that I propose."

"Hard limits?"

"Things that you are not willing to do. Please feel free to add anything else you can think of."

NO DEFECATION OR URINATION.

No blood.

No medical instruments of any kind.

No illegal acts of any kind.

No acts that will leave a permanent mark on the skin.

I STARE at the list of hard limits. None of them even seem like something anyone would want to do. I don't really know why they need to be specifically outlined in a contract.

"What do you think?" Aiden asks, handing me a pen.

But I shake my head. Suddenly, a fun trip on a luxurious super-yacht doesn't seem that appealing after all.

"Are you okay?" he asks after a moment.

I shake my head.

"No, I don't think so."

"What's wrong?"

"Nothing." I shrug my shoulder. But that's a lie. The truth is that I can't do this.

"I'm not this person," I say after a while. "The thing is that I'm not someone who wants to sign any sort of contract to have sex with a man I love."

Aiden looks away, running his fingers through his hair.

"I didn't mean to offend you."

"You didn't."

"Clearly, I did."

"Well, maybe a little," I say. "But it doesn't matter."

He takes the contract and rips it up.

"What are you doing?"

"The thing is that was just for fun," he says with a shrug. "The truth is that I want to be with you. That's all."

"Without any paperwork?"

"Without any paperwork."

My eyes light up at the thought. I want to be with him, too. And actually, I wouldn't mind doing something a little bit more adventurous sexually. I just don't think I want to put it on paper.

CHAPTER 7 - ELLIE

WHEN NIGHT TURNS INTO DAY…

Aiden takes me into his arms and presses his lips to mine.

"I'm sorry," I whisper. "It just threw me for a loop a bit."

"It's okay, I understand. It's not for everyone."

"Can we try something else then?" he asks after a moment.

My heart sinks into my stomach. I'm scared to disappoint him again, but there's no way I'm going to do anything that I don't want to do.

"Okay," I say, tentatively.

Without another word, Aiden takes my hand and leads me to the far end of his stateroom, to his private bathroom.

The bathroom is modern in every sense of the word. Everything is white on white on gray. Contemporary finishes and white stone with sparkling inlays. The large tub at the end of the room, by the bay window, is deep, egg-shaped, and claw footed. It's one of those old-fashioned tubs which are completely brand new. Aiden leans over and turns on the faucet, which sits comfortably in the middle of the tub. He drops a large bath bomb into the water and the whole room explodes with the aroma of lavender and honey.

Aiden takes off his t-shirt and peels off his tight jeans. When he approaches, I become keenly aware of just how fully dressed I am.

"Will you let me bathe you?" he asks. I take a step back, wrapping my arms around myself as tightly as I can. We have been intimate many times before, and yet this feels like it will be more intimate than anything else that we have done.

"I don't know," I say.

"Are you serious?" He laughs.

"I know, it's silly right?" I shrug. "But…bathe me? Why do you want to bathe me?"

"Because I want to drape your beautiful body with water. I want to see you."

Shivers run up my spine. He dims the lights until the room is lit up by candlelight. I admire his chiseled physique. Each muscle in his body protrudes with each breath, calling me to him. I press my fingers against his six pack and run them over each individual muscle group.

"Oh, no," Aiden whispers, pushing my hands back.

"What?"

"You can't touch me unless you get into the bath."

"What?" I ask, smiling.

"What's fair is fair. I want you. And I can tell that you want me, too. But I'm not giving you what you want unless I get a little of what I want."

I shake my head. Then something occurs to me. I push up my shirt and reveal my stomach. He stares at my midriff until I drop my shirt back down.

"There. You got something."

Aiden starts to laugh. A deep, bellowing laugh that fills my whole body with joy.

"What? Was that not enough for you?" I ask. He shakes his head and grabs me.

"Hell, no."

With one swift motion, he throws me gently into the water. It takes me a moment to even realize what has happened.

"Oh my God! I'm wet!"

"More like soaking wet."

I splash the water at him, but it's not much of a deterrent. Instead, he simply kneels down next to me and smiles that beautiful smile of his. I laugh as well, as the water seeps into every part of me. My jeans feel incredibly heavy and my shirt clings to every part of me.

"I can't believe you did that," I say, pushing my hair to the top of my head and tying a loose knot.

"I love you," Aiden whispers, brushing some water from my face. "I love you very much."

"I love you, too."

"Now that you're wet, we're going to have to do something about these clothes." He tugs at my shirt and pulls it over my head. I consider protesting, but the warm water and his gorgeous body are just too hard to pass up. I give in and let him undress me. Pulling off my jeans proves to be a much harder process, but with a little bit of help from me, he eventually succeeds.

"You should've let me undress you when you were dry," Aiden says.

"Yeah, maybe. But it wouldn't have been nearly as much fun."

My bra and panties slip off much more easily and I'm left entirely naked before him. Even though he looks at me with nothing but love and admiration, I am very well aware of my own flaws. Maybe a little bit too aware. There's the pouch under my belly button that's a bit too big and my thighs, which could use a little toning. My body is nothing like those his previous dates had - all those models and actresses he bedded. Yet, he barely notices. In fact, he doesn't seem to notice at all.

"Look at me," Aiden says, putting his index finger under my chin. "Why the sad face?"

"I'm just a little...uncomfortable," I say, covering my stomach with my arms. I'm not sure why I'm feeling particularly vulnerable right now. Perhaps, it's the warm weather and the hot bath - they tend to showcase a lot of imperfections.

"You shouldn't. You are beautiful and I want to spend my days staring at your gorgeous body."

I nod and let my arms go. It feels nice to give in and not worry so much. As I move my hands around in the hot water and relax, bubbles finally start to build up from the bath bomb. Within a few moments, the entire tub is filled with effervescent round circles of soap.

"Close your eyes."

When I do as he says, a stream of hot water rushes down my face. Aiden's squeezing a sponge over my head. Losing myself in the moment, I lie back in the tub and surrender. Slowly, Aiden dips the sponge under the water and runs it over my neck, breasts and stomach. Carefully, he takes each arm out of the water and runs the sponge over it, back and forth.

"This feels so good."

"I'm glad."

A few moments later, he stops. I open my eyes and look up at him with disappointment.

"Oh, I see, you seem to have enjoyed that."

"Yes, I did."

"Didn't you say you didn't want to get bathed?"

"I guess I was wrong."

Aiden gives me a brief kiss on the lips before asking, "Mind if I join you?"

I shake my head no.

I move a little to make room, but the tub is so big and deep that there's plenty of room for both of us.

Aiden lowers himself in front of me. I pick up some water in my hands and run it over his neck, watching it scroll down. He reaches for some body wash behind him and lathers it up in his hands. Then he rubs the soft foam into my shoulders.

I close my eyes. He runs his hands over my breasts,

pausing briefly at my nipples. It tickles and I laugh a little.

I take some of the foam off my body and place it on his, rubbing gently as I make my way down his neck and back, submerging my fingers into the water.

I lean toward him and press my lips to his. He pulls me closer. He is in control now and I surrender. I love the feel of his hands all over me, directing me into whatever direction he wants to take me. He wraps my legs around his and pushes my hair away from my neck.

Shivers run down my spine as he positions my body on top of his. I press my legs tightly to him as he takes my butt into his hands. He smiles and gives me a flirtatious squeeze. Slowly, he lowers me on top of him and pushes himself deep inside. I feel as if my body is being pierced through and I let myself go.

"I love being inside of you," he whispers as our bodies become one. Intertwined, he presses his lips onto mine and then parts them forcefully with his tongue.

I moan and bury my hands in his hair. I need to be even closer to him. My body starts to move up and down as if on its own. Despite the fact that I have him, I want him. All of him. Our kisses become more frantic. He pulls on my hair with his hands and I moan and toss my head back in ecstasy.

He's holding me up and guiding my movements. I slide up and down his large cock and my body starts to swell from the pleasure that's building up in between my legs. When he finds my clit and rubs against it as well, I can't contain anything within me anymore.

"Aiden!" I moan into his ear. A few moments later, while I'm still riding the high of my climax, he reaches his.

"I...love...you," he mumbles as he moves faster and faster in and out of me until he finally collapses underneath me.

We sit in the tub, with our bodies intertwined together, until the water turns cold. This actually takes a while since the tub is quite expensive and is made from some material with great insulation.

"I've never had sex in the water before," I say.

"How was it?"

"Perfect."

The water slowly runs out of heat, and yet both Aiden and I refuse to move a muscle. I don't know what he's thinking, but I feel as if I'm under a spell. If I were to make a move to get out, the whole moment would shatter and would make it as if none of this had never happened.

CHAPTER 8 - ELLIE

THE ANSWER...

The following morning, I wake up in Aiden's arms. The light is just peeking through the windows. It's warm out and we are covered only by a sheet, and that's enough. I have to pinch myself to make sure that this moment is real. Am I really lying next to the man of my dreams on a beautiful yacht in the middle of the warm Caribbean when it's below freezing back home?

I look over at him. He's barely stirring.

"I love you," I whisper. He smiles without opening his eyes.

"I love you, too," he mumbles.

I stare at his tan skin and chiseled jaw, waiting for him to wake up. A few moments later, he finally looks at me.

"You know, I can feel you staring at me," he says.

"I know."

Aiden stretches his arms above his head and arches his back. The sheet falls to the side, exposing my breasts and his perfect six pack. I run my fingers down his abs and lick my lips.

"You're going to kill me, woman."

"Hey, I'm just enjoying the moment. Not instigating anything, right?"

"Yeah, right." He laughs. "Okay, fine, since you're up and wide awake, I have something to ask you."

With one swift motion, he climbs on top of me and cradles my face in between his arms.

"What?"

Aiden pulls the sheet over us, making a little cocoon. Now, we are in our own little world, away from everything that's horrible and wrong.

"You are the most beautiful woman in the world," Aiden says. "But that's not why I want to ask you this.'

"Okay..."

"Ellie, whenever I'm around you, I want to be a better version of myself. You make me want to be a better man. And that's why I want to ask you to be my wife."

I stare at him, dumbfounded.

"Will you marry me, Ellie?"

The last time the answer came so easily. I just looked into his eyes and the answer just spilled out. But now? I don't know why, but I feel myself hesitating. It has nothing to do with the moment. This place, this setting, is perfect. And yet, I can't bring myself to say yes.

"I don't know," I say. Aiden's mouth drops open in disappointment.

"Why?"

"I don't know. I mean, I said yes before and then

everything just sort of got so complicated and now...
now, I don't know."

He nods as if he understands, but he doesn't. I barely
understand it myself. I have no idea why I'm saying
no except that there's this voice inside of me that's
telling me that this isn't right. Not right now. I mean,
I love him. I really do. And I want to spend all of my
time with him. But I don't know if I can commit to be
his wife. Not yet.

"I don't know if you know this, but I never really
wanted to get married. I mean, little girls grow up
imagining what their weddings will be like and
where they will go on a honeymoon. But I was never
like that. Marriage always felt a little bit like a trap. I
mean, I have no problem making a commitment to
you. I love you. It's just the wedding and everything
that goes along with it."

Aiden listens and nods. "Well, just know that there's
no pressure. I mean, we don't have to have a big
ceremony, if that's what's freaking you out. We don't
even have to invite anyone if you don't want to. We
can just elope. Or not."

Hmm, elope. That does sound nice.

"You mean, just go to the courthouse and that's it?"

He nods.

"Maybe. That does make me feel a little better." He smiles at me and gives me a warm hug.

"I never thought I wanted to get married again," Aiden says after a while. "I mean, my first time wasn't amazing so I was sort of over the whole thing. But then I met you. And it's not like I want to pin you down to anything. I just want to tell you that I want to be with you. That's all. Forever. And if that doesn't mean marriage to you, that's fine. I'm totally fine with that. I'm happy as long as you want to spend your life with me."

"I do. Very much so," I say, giving him a big kiss.

A private ceremony. I never really considered that before, but why not? No big dress, no huge wedding that would make me the center of attention. Now, that sounds more like it.

"I'm not sure Caroline would approve," I joke.

"Of what?"

"Of a courthouse wedding. She loves lavish parties

and any reason to get dressed up. I think she will kill me if we just go to the courthouse in jeans."

"Well, it's not her wedding, is it?"

"No, it's not."

I sit up in bed and look out at the bright blue ocean outside the balcony. Perhaps, the thing that makes me not want to get married is the party itself. I mean, being with Aiden for the rest of my life? I can make that commitment in a second. It's a no-brainer. I love him and I want to be with him every waking hour of every day. But hosting a lavish wedding where I am the center of attention? Most women would love that. All eyes on them, celebrating their beauty. But me? No, that's not my cup of tea. In fact, I usually go out of my way not to have attention on me. That's why I write under a pseudonym. I like my life private.

"Ellie?"

"Yes?"

"I just want to be with you. For however long you will have me. And if you don't want to get married, that's totally fine. And if you change your mind, that's fine, too. I won't ask you anymore as long as you promise me one thing."

"What's that?"

"That you will stay with me as long as you love me and not a minute longer."

"What do you mean?" I ask, taken a little aback by this statement.

"I never want to be one of those couples that are together just because they've invested too much time in their relationship. I love you. And I believe I always will. I know you love me and I think you always will. But, if for some reason, you suddenly don't. Like in a year or ten or fifty. It doesn't matter. If you don't love me anymore, then I want you to leave. You deserve to be happy and if that's not with me, then I want you to go out and find someone you will love with all of your heart. I want you to be happy, Ellie."

I smile. He presses his lips to mine and I lose myself in the kiss.

CHAPTER 9 - ELLIE

THE ISLAND...

The following morning, Aiden docks the yacht at the far end of a tiny limestone island called Caye Caulker. Caye is pronounced like Key as in the Florida Keys, but spelled differently. It's about two miles across, and belongs to Belize, a small nation in Central America of about 300,000 people. Belize is bordered by Guatemala and Mexico to the north and is popular with many American expats because it's the only English speaking nation south of the United States.

I walk down the wooden dock and admire the sweeping palm trees which bend in the gentle breeze coming off-shore.

"This place is breathtaking," I whisper as I take off my flip-flops and bury my feet in the white sand. The island is so tiny that there are no proper roads or cars. According to Aiden, the nearby island called Ambergris Caye is much more populated and developed and the main mode of transportation there is the golf cart.

We walk down Front Street, one of the three mains streets, which runs right along the shoreline. Since there are no cars or even golf carts, the only sounds I hear belong to laughing people and chirping birds.

"This place is...amazing," I say, stopping at one of the booths where a woman in a long floral dress is selling coconut water. Aiden and I order two. She takes the fresh green coconut, puts it on a tree stump, and pulls out a giant machete. With one expert swing, the top of the coconut drops to the ground. She places a straw into the opening and hands it to me.

"This is delicious!" I say, taking another long sip. "I've never had fresh coconut water before."

"Once you have this, you'll never be able to drink that coconut water they sell in the States again,"

Aiden says. "No matter how much they tell you that it's fresh, you'll know it isn't."

I totally agree with him.

"I've never been a fan of coconuts before because of their strange aftertaste. Like all those coconut flakes they sell that everyone loves? You know what I mean?"

"Yes. That aftertaste means it's old. Dated."

"But this fresh coconut water…I just can't get enough." I drink the coconut dry and stop at another booth for second helpings.

A few minutes later, we reach the end of Front Street. It runs straight into the water. Apparently, this is the end of the island.

"This area is called the Split," Aiden says. "You see that island across the way? In the 60's, a big hurricane came through and blew this place in half."

I look across the water. It's not a long way over, but it's definitely not very close either. On the other side, by the mangroves, I see a bunch of kids swinging and jumping into the water.

"No one really lives over there. They're selling some lots as this place is getting more popular, but there aren't any buildings there. No electricity, of course, or any other conveniences."

"So, how did those kids get over there?"

"They swam."

I look at the Split and over at the kids and back again. Some of them are barely five years old and there are no adults in sight.

"They must be great swimmers," I point.

"If you grow up around here, you kind of have to be," Aiden says. "C'mon, let's get a drink."

We walk over to the bar, right at the edge of the water, called the Lazy Lizard. it's a big wooden structure with a bar top, bottled beer, and nothing but sand underneath the wooden barstools. I take off my flip-flops and bury my feet in the sand.

"This feels nice."

Aiden gives me a kiss on the cheek. He hands me my beer and leads me to the dock at the Split. There are people sunbathing all around, with kids jumping into the water right from the dock. This part of the island doesn't have a sandy beach and the water gets twenty feet deep right away. I find a spot on the dock, hang my feet off the side, and take a sip of the light Belizean beer called Belkin. The warm salt air seems to fill every part of me and makes me more awake than I ever was before.

At this place, at the edge of a dock, on a small island in the middle of the Caribbean, the world seems to be entirely different. Time moves at a different pace and the pressures and realities of my old life simply vanish. After jumping in and swimming around in the warm water, Aiden and I come back up to sunbathe.

"I have to tell you something," Aiden says after we've been lying in the sun for who knows how long.

"Hmmm," I mumble, unable to move. I need to go back into the water, but I'm too hot to move. Aiden seems to be similarly relaxed.

"My attorney got wind that Blake might not be working out."

This piques my attention. I ask him for the details, but he doesn't really have many. There are rumors that Blake isn't doing well as interim CEO, but they need a good reason to get rid of him.

I can't stand the heat anymore. I jump off the dock and submerge myself in the clear blue water. I'm a pretty good swimmer so treading water doesn't take much effort for me.

"Aiden, I was thinking, maybe it's time I made a report about what happened. What Blake did to me."

Aiden dives off the dock.

"What kind of report?" he asks when he comes back up.

"Police report. I mean, it didn't happen that long ago. And the main reason I didn't do it before was that I was worried what would happen to your job if the auction thing came out. But now, it's sort of out already."

"I don't know, Ellie. Only if you want to. I don't want you to do it for me. Not at all. It needs to be entirely your decision."

"Is there any reason why you wouldn't want me to go public with this?"

"No." Aiden shakes his head. "Frankly, I never wanted you to keep it quiet on my behalf. That guy is an asshole and pretty dangerous. I hate the fact that you felt like you needed to keep this quiet on my behalf. Fuck my career, if that means keeping a criminal like him off the streets."

I admire his passion. Of course, I doubt that he would get any jail time for what he did to me. He would get a great lawyer and so much time has passed that I'm not sure anything is provable anymore. But still, it might make things uncomfortable. Maybe, it will even get him kicked out of his job. I doubt that it will get Aiden his job back, but the world deserves to know that Blake is a sexual assaulter. He is someone who will take advantage of a woman in a vulnerable situation. He thought that by doing what he did where he did, I would be too embarrassed or ashamed to come forward. Well, perhaps I was, at first. But now that some of that story is out already, I have nothing to lose. I have a voice and I'm going to set the record straight.

I swim around for a while mulling this over. When I climb back onto the dock, I've made up my mind.

"I'm going to press charges when we get back," I say. "I'm not letting him get away with this."

CHAPTER 10 - AIDEN

THE ISLAND

O ver an early dinner of fresh fish and large island cocktails, I ask Ellie to clarify what she said earlier on the dock. The sun was beating down hard out there and I'm not entirely sure that I heard her correctly. Did she really say that she wanted go public with what Blake did to her? Go to the police?

"Yes, I do. I wasn't kidding," Ellie says, burying her feet further in the sand under the bench. A soft cool breeze comes off the ocean, adding some zest to my already perfect ceviche.

"I don't want you to do it just for me," I say. "It won't change my situation at all."

"Oh, that's not why," she says. "I've just been reading the news and I'm really inspired by all of these women coming forward and calling their abusers out on all the shit that they have done to them. Frankly, I don't really care if no one believes me. I just want it to be out in the open. I want him to be embarrassed over what he did. That's the least that could happen to him."

I doubt that he will be embarrassed, but at least he will be uncomfortable. I am almost one hundred percent positive that he will deny that any of that ever happened and try to start a smear campaign against me and what happened at the auction on my yacht. Oh, well. If this is what Ellie wants to do, I'm going to support her. Frankly, she should've done this originally. I shouldn't have let her cover up his crime on my account and I feel like a total shit for even entertaining the notion.

"So, how do I do this?" Ellie asks. "I mean, where do I start? Do I go straight to the police?"

"I don't really know. But it's probably best to contact an attorney first. See what they say."

"I don't know any attorneys."

"Feel free to use any of mine. God knows I have enough. We'll see what they say and then maybe make a statement through them. I think they can contact the police on your behalf but you will have to talk to the cops directly as well. I don't think you'll get away with just a statement since you're planning on pressing charges."

"That's okay, I sort of expected that."

My phone rings. "Oh, I'm sorry, I thought I had turned it off."

It's sitting on the bench in between us and Ellie looks down at the screen.

"Leslie PR," she reads the name that flashes on the screen. "Is she your public relations person?"

I nod.

"Do you mind if I talk to her?"

I shrug. Wow, she's more serious about this than I had thought.

Ellie picks up the phone, puts Leslie on speaker, and

introduces herself. Without letting Leslie get a word in edgewise - and trust me, that's a pretty hard thing to do - she goes into the story about Blake and what happened back at the yacht. It covers it pretty succinctly, using big brushstrokes, but without leaving any of the important details out. At the end, she tells her that she has talked it over with me and she would like to press charges.

"Really, Aiden?" Leslie asks. "Is this really happening?"

Her voice is a little bit more elated than it probably should be, given the topic of the conversation, but Leslie can't help but be excited about the latest gossip. And knowing ahead of time that Blake Garrison, the CEO of Owl, is being accused of sexual assault is as juicy as it gets.

"Yes, unfortunately it is."

"Well, I do wish that you had told me about this sooner, but I understand why you didn't. You are just like the rest of my clients."

"Before the Page Six article came out, I thought I could just let this go," Ellie explains. "Having an auction on your yacht isn't exactly acceptable behavior for someone who runs a Fortune 500 company, even though my readers seem to be really into the concept."

"So, everything in that article is true?"

"Yes." Ellie nods even though Leslie can't see her. "But now that so many other stories about women who have been assaulted are coming forward and telling the world about them being assaulted, I don't want to keep this quiet anymore. That man needs to pay for what he has done. I'm not going to be complicit in lying to the world on his behalf. No matter what it costs me."

I squeeze Ellie's hand. Her bravery is awe-inspiring. Imagining what Blake did to her on the yacht, the way he took advantage of her, sends hatred coursing through my veins. I hate him. I despise him with every fiber of my being. I want to see him burn. Now I know how incredibly selfish I was in even letting her keep this quiet on my behalf. I didn't ask her to and I would've never asked her not to go to the police, but I didn't exactly encourage her to come forward. I let her hide away. I let Blake's horrible deed stay quiet. I helped him bury it and, for that, I will not be able to forgive myself for a very long time.

"So, what do you recommend we do now?" I ask.

Leslie thinks about it for a moment.

"Since you are set on pressing charges, I recommend you, Ellie, file a police report as soon as possible. And retain an attorney."

I thank her for her time and promise to get in touch soon. She will be the first to know when Ellie is ready to go public with this so that she can use her public relations magic to get the story told right.

"As soon as Blake finds out about this, his people will start an all-out smear campaign against you, Ellie, and Aiden. They will publish the worst things you can imagine about both of you individually and as a couple. I just want you to be ready for that. I need you to prepare yourselves psychologically for that," Leslie warns.

"We'll be ready," Ellie says confidently.

"I will do my best to get ahead of whatever stories that they may come up with, but I want you both to be prepared that there will be stories about you.

Discrediting you will be the only way that he can wrangle himself out of this."

"Do you think you'll be able to handle this?" I ask Ellie after she hangs up the phone.

"Yes."

"To take on Blake? And his public relations smear team?"

"Yes. Don't you think I can handle this?"

"Of course, I do. I just wish I could protect you from all the shit that they're going to pile on you. But I don't think I will be able to."

"I'm a big girl, Aiden."

"Yes, I know that. But still, I'm not sure you will be prepared for this. I'm not sure I will either."

I give her a brief peck on the lips. I want to protect her from everything bad that the world will throw at her, but I know that I can't.

"Let's not talk about this anymore," Ellie says, finishing her drink. "I want to have another cocktail, take a walk along the beach with you, and then take you back to your yacht."

The tone in her voice indicates that she has something sultry in mind for tonight.

"Oh, really?" I ask.

She nods and licks her lips in a sensual way that makes my cock get hard.

CHAPTER 11 - ELLIE

After a long stroll under the moonlight with our flip-flops in our hands, Aiden takes me back to his yacht. The island is small, with a population of less than two thousand people, the majority of whom go to bed by ten o'clock at night. There are no wild parties and even the couple of bars that do exist tend to close early. As we walk back to the boat, it feels like we have the whole island to ourselves.

"I love it here," I say. "Though to tell you the truth, I was expecting it to be a little bit more hopping at night."

"Oh, that's the funny part about this place. Since

everyone wakes up so early to build lobster pods and go fishing or diving, all the locals tend to retire to bed pretty early. But they are up early as well."

"How early?" I ask.

"Like six. Sometimes five-thirty."

"That's insane!"

"Well, not if you're in bed by eleven."

I shake my head. Unlike most people my age, I require a lot of sleep. And by that, I mean a lot. Like nine or ten hours a night. I used to think I needed that much sleep because I was depressed, but I've been this way almost my whole life, so I got pretty used to it.

"So, they don't consider getting up at eight-thirty early in these parts?" I ask, squeezing his hand. Aiden, who is well-familiar with my nighttime habits, shakes his head and laughs.

He leads me down the dock and onto the yacht. He told the staff that there was no need to wait up for us and we head straight to the master suite. We haven't discussed it much after we talked to Leslie, but I know that I have to make the police report sometime soon and that means that I have to go back to New York. Perhaps even as early as tomorrow. And even if we don't head back right away, I will probably have to have an extensive conversation with one or more of his attorneys tomorrow so that they can start the ball rolling on this whole thing. At this moment, I suddenly wish that none of this was happening anymore. I just want to stay in Caye Caulker forever, or at least for a month or two and pretend that no world outside of this little limestone island off the coast of Central America exists.

"One last thought about this whole pressing charges thing," Aiden says. "Please don't be pressured to move forward with this any sooner than you feel like you want to. There's absolutely no rush."

"Thanks. I appreciate it. But the sooner I get this ball rolling, the sooner it will be over, right?"

Aiden shrugs. "I guess, in theory. But, in reality? Who the hell knows?"

"I don't want to talk about this anymore tonight," I say, sitting down on the bed. "I just want you to fuck me."

"Oh, really?" he asks. I clearly caught him off guard.

"Yes, please."

CHAPTER 12 - ELLIE

In the morning, Aiden puts me on the phone with two of his attorneys and I tell them what Blake did to me during the party. They take careful notes and ask me about a zillion questions. They also develop a plan of action. They ask when is the soonest that I can come back to New York and file a police report. I need to put all of this on record before they can proceed with filing charges. Since it didn't happen that long ago, there's still time to press criminal charges before going after him civilly. This is the best course of action, according to the attorneys. They don't say this, but I know that this will also likely confirm his firing as the interim CEO of Owl. If the Board of Directors isn't happy with him now, they definitely won't be happy with this turn of events. This isn't exactly why I'm so eager to file a report against Blake, but it's definitely a cherry on top. He took my boyfriend's job and I like having the power to oust him from that position, or at least do something to contribute to the firing.

Over breakfast, Aiden and I decide that the best thing to do now would be to just go back to New York. With his access to a helicopter and a private plane, we aren't subject to regular flight schedules and Aiden thinks that we can file a report, brief the attorneys, and get back to sitting with our feet in the sand and cocktails in our hands on Caye Caulker within twenty-four hours. That seems like wishful thinking to me, but I'm definitely hoping to be back in forty-eight hours.

The flights back to New York are rather uneventful. I ask Aiden to stay behind and enjoy his yacht, but he doesn't want to hear anything about it. He wants to be there to hold my hand and I appreciate it. The closer we get to New York, the more freaked out I get over going to the police station and making a report. Somehow, in the middle of the Caribbean, this whole situation didn't seem quite as real as it does when we land back on the ground.

We head straight from the airport to the police precinct. Thanks to Aiden's attorneys, the cops there are aware of our coming and are prepared for us. They take me back to a special room, tell me that the video camera is on, and ask me to make a statement. The room doesn't have one of those two-way mirrors I've seen in the movies. But it is just as claustrophobic, windowless, and bland as I expected. There isn't one interesting thing to look at on the walls. They are completely bare. I sit behind a plain dark wood table on one of the most uncomfortable chairs I've ever had the displeasure of using.

I point this out to the cop, and tell him that they remind me of the kind of chair I had my freshman year at Yale, but he doesn't really commiserate. Instead, he asks me to start at the beginning. How I got to the party? What was actually taking place at the auction? I nod and say that I will as soon as my attorney gets here.

Aiden and I have talked this over. This is quite sensitive information, as you can imagine. The idea that someone is hosting an auction of attractive girls off the coast of New York isn't exactly something that isn't going to pique the police's interest. But Aiden insisted that I need to tell them everything. That's the only way that my name, which will undoubtedly be speared anyway, won't be able to be badmouthed completely.

"I have to tell them the truth," he said.

"But wouldn't that make what you were doing...illegal?"

"No, not necessarily."

"Of course, it will. I mean, there was an exchange. These men are paying for sex and you're orchestrating the whole thing."

We had to turn to his attorney to settle the argument. He said that I would have to use very specific language to not make it prostitution and that I was not to utter a single world without his presence.

There's a knock at the door. When the cop answers, an attractive guy in his late thirties comes in wearing an immaculate suit and carrying an expensive looking briefcase. Everything about him is polished, from his $400 haircut down to his $700 shoes. He introduces himself as Neil Goss, my attorney. So, this

was the guy we talked to on the phone last night.
Hmm. Really didn't expect him to be so easy on
the eyes.

Officer Lindon shakes his hand and gives him a seat
at the table. Then he excuses himself to get another
chair.

"Are you ready?" Neil asks.

"I think so."

"Just say what we practiced this morning. If you have
any doubts about what you should or shouldn't say,
don't say a word and confirm it with me."

When Officer Lindon returns, I start at the
beginning. I start with my roommate, Caroline,
inviting me to a yacht party - the first time I met
Aiden. The cop asks me all sorts of questions about
the boat and how I got there prior to getting to the
auction. He's warming me up and it's working. My
words flow a little bit smoother and I relax a bit.
Finally, it's time to describe the auction. I look over
at Neil, who gets a little tense in between his
shoulders but otherwise covers up his discomfort
very well. Without further ado, I dive right in and
explain it, just as we had practiced it earlier.

"So, these women are basically getting sold to the highest bidder?" Officer Lindon asks. He's trying to throw me off, sidetrack me. But I won't let him.

"No, the bidding is just for fun. The men pay money to basically meet the girls and spend time with them. But sex isn't part of the exchange."

"So, you and the other girls didn't have sex with the men who bid on you?"

"My client does not have any knowledge about what the other women at the party did or did not do afterward," Neil interrupts.

"Okay, what about you, Ellie?"

"Well, yes, Aiden and I were intimate. But it had nothing to do with the money."

"No?"

"No." I shake my head. "I'm not a prostitute. The auction was just a fancy introduction service. It's really a way for rich powerful men to show off how much money they can spend on a hot girl. But there's no required reciprocity. If any of the women did have sex with the men who bid on them, they did it purely because they wanted to. Just like me."

Officer Lindon doesn't entirely buy this. But I try to
steer the conversation to my second trip to the yacht
and what Blake did. I'm not the one who is on trial
here. I'm a victim. Luckily, Lindon doesn't object.

Five hours later, I'm finally free to go. After
explaining the whole situation in detail and getting
it all on tape, Officer Lindon asked me to write down
my complaint and sign it as well. Prior to signing,
Neil carefully read all five pages of my complaint
against Blake, scrutinizing each word. In a few
instances, he asked me to change a few words - to be
more vague - and in a few, he asked me to be more
precise.

"I had no idea that words were so important in your
profession," I say, signing each page of my statement.

"Words are everything. Or rather the way that words
are interpreted. What else is there, right?"

That's a nice way to think about it. I've been
conditioned to think that being an English major
was a pretty useless degree, but not to Neil. All
English majors do is analyze text and words and
apparently, that's all Neil does in his job as well.

After we hand over my statement, I'm free to go.

Aiden meets us on the curb in his car. He's going to make his statement tomorrow. Even though it's dark already, Neil refuses a ride and instead hails a cab. I bid him farewell and climb into Aiden's car.

"How did it go?"

"Long. I'm so tired."

"I can imagine."

"Be prepared for a very tedious examination."

Aiden nods and squeezes my hand. We are planning on taking off right after Aiden gives his statement tomorrow. Neither of us want to hang around New York when the story breaks and becomes news, which it will undoubtedly become with Leslie on our side. Everything else can be handled through lawyers and public relations executives. If there's a trial then we will both come back, prepare, and testify, but until then, there's no reason to hang around here.

"I can't wait to get back to Caye Caulker," I whisper when he pulls up to my apartment. I'm going to stay at my place tonight. Aiden's meeting with the cops early tomorrow morning and he's going to pick me up as soon as he's done so we can head back down to the Caribbean.

"Me neither," he says, stopping the car at the curb and giving me a big kiss on the lips.

"See you tomorrow," I say and get out.

CHAPTER 13 - ELLIE

R iding up the elevator, I'm excited to see Caroline again. I feel bad about how I left things and I hope she didn't go to her parents' yet. I'd love to have a fun evening watching something funny. I unlock the door and call her name. No answer. Shit. I guess she left already. I drop my bag on the floor in front of the kitchen island and knock on her bedroom door. No answer again.

I turn the knob slowly. I don't want to wake her in case she's sleeping.

When I open the door, I immediately feel like something's wrong. I see her lying spread-eagle on her back on top of the covers. She's wearing her pajamas and her arms and legs are spread wide open. She looks as if she might be asleep, but I've never seen her sleep that way before.

"Oh my God...Caroline! Caroline!" I run over to the bed. I shake her, trying to rouse her. I turn her head and see that there's vomit around her mouth and on the bedspread.

"Caroline, Caroline, please!" I yell. My whole body starts to shake as I pull her down to the floor and start doing CPR. "Please wake up, please wake up."

I press down on her chest three times in quick succession. I wipe her mouth with the back of my hand, cover her nose, and breathe into her mouth. I don't know if this is the right way of doing it. Something in the back of my head says that they no longer advise to breathe into the mouth to revive people, but I have no idea if I'm remembering that right. I continue to press down on her chest and breathe into her mouth because that's what I've seen people do in movies and right now I'm at a total loss as to what else to do. Without stopping CPR, I dial 911.

"Please help. I came home and my roommate is unresponsive on the floor. It looks like she passed out and threw up and now I can't wake her."

My voice is rushed and frantic, but the older woman's soothing voice on the other line puts me somewhat at ease. She asks for my address and dispatches officers and an ambulance. Then she asks me to do CPR. I tell her that I have been without much response.

"Just keep doing that until someone gets there. They aren't far away."

I hear their sirens in the distance. A minute later, they burst through the door, which I luckily forgot to lock behind me. I hang up the phone as soon as our apartment fills with people. A police officer helps me up as the paramedics start to work on her and leads me to the living room.

She starts asking me questions, which I answer completely in a daze. All of my thoughts keep focusing on Caroline. Please be okay, I chant over and over. Please, be okay. You have to be okay.

Tears are welling up in the back of my eyes and I try

to keep them at bay. The police officer puts her arm around me, but it only makes me feel more alone.

More and more people stream into her bedroom and come out with grave expressions on their faces.

"What's going on?" I ask. The cop keeps asking me questions, but I no longer answer them. I've told her enough and now I need some answers myself. Just as I'm about to go back into Caroline's room, the paramedics come out with the gurney. But instead of seeing Caroline's sweet face, all I see is her body in a bag.

"What's going on?" I ask. "Caroline? Why do you have this bag zipped up? She can't breathe!"

I become hysterical. Whatever tears I managed to keep at bay thus far, break free and stream down my face. I try to push my way to her. I need to unzip that bag. I need to help her breathe. But they're not letting me. They're blocking me.

"You're killing her!" I scream. "You're killing her. She can't breathe like that."

"I'm so sorry, honey," someone says to me in a low voice. "She's dead. She's dead."

Everything turns black. Nothing makes sense anymore. I see people moving all around me, but they're no longer real. They are just copies of people. Actors maybe. Maybe none of this is real after all. How can it be? How can the world go on without Caroline in it? My sweet, funny, kind Caroline?

THEY TAKE Caroline's body from our apartment and it's as if she has gone to her parents. Her clothes are still hanging in her closet and her room is just as she has left it. It feels like she just stepped out, or maybe went away on a short trip. It definitely doesn't feel like she's dead. And yet, that's what she is. At least, that's what they say.

Aiden is in the kitchen making me tea. Someone called him using my phone. He came over after they wheeled Caroline away. There are no more police or paramedics in my apartment. They did their jobs and went on their way to some other emergency. They did what they were supposed to do and now I'm left here picking up the pieces. All alone. Well, not all alone, but it surely does feel that way. Aiden isn't Caroline and he never will be. No matter what he says or doesn't say, she's not coming back.

He offers me a cup of tea, but I no longer want it. It doesn't feel right to have tea when she's gone. It doesn't feel right to do anything when she's no longer here. I go to my room and climb into bed.

CHAPTER 14 - ELLIE

WHEN EVERYTHING TURNS TO BLACK...

When I wake up, it's morning again. As soon as I open my eyes, I can't breathe again. The world just chokes me up. Tears start flowing and nothing makes sense. How can I continue living without Caroline? How can the world continue spinning without her in it? No, I can't deal with it. I close my eyes again.

A few hours later, I wake up and this time I can't make it go away. No matter how much I try to push the whole world away, I can't. I can't sleep anymore. And I can't cry anymore either. No, the only thing I can do is just lose myself in the numbness. I hate it and I hate myself and yet nothing changes despite all of this hate.

"Hi," I say quietly. Aiden is in the kitchen with his head stuck in his phone.

"Oh my God, you're up. How are you?"

I look at the clock above the stove. It's two in the afternoon.

"Wow, I slept late."

"Yes, but that's ok. You needed the rest."

"It doesn't seem right."

"What do you mean?"

"To sleep, after your best friend dies."

"Oh, honey," Aiden says, putting his arm around me and giving me a squeeze. Even though I feel his touch and his warm body next to mine, it doesn't seem real. It's as if I'm watching someone else getting a hug, someone on television. I feel the warmth emanating from him, but it doesn't reach me, because he's not real. Or is it me who's not real? I don't really know.

"Did I make that statement to the police yesterday?" I ask.

"Yes, last night."

"Did you go this morning?"

"No," Aiden says, looking away. "I rescheduled."

"Why?"

"I wanted to stay here with you. I didn't want you to wake up to an empty apartment all by yourself."

I shrug. More tears will start flowing eventually, but for now I don't have any more left.

"Do you want me to make you some breakfast? Eggs? Or maybe pancakes?"

I shake my head no. My mouth is completely dry, parched. And there's not one thing that I can do about it.

"Then have this at least," Aiden says, handing me a granola bar. "I want you to eat something to keep up your strength."

I stare at him. A minute later, I open the wrapper and take a bite. It tastes so dry that I choke on it. He hands me a glass of water and I let the cold liquid run down my throat. Suddenly, I am keenly aware of every last sensation around me. I take another bite of the granola bar, but much to my surprise, I can't taste it. It tastes like cardboard. It is completely devoid of flavor.

"I'm going back to bed," I say. I know that I have to engage more with him. I need to ask him what happened to Caroline, whether anyone told her parents. I need to start making plans or helping her mother and her family make plans for the funeral, but I can't deal with any of that now. In fact, I kind of doubt that I will ever be able to deal with it.

THE NEXT FEW days after Caroline's death proceed pretty much like the other one. I'm in a daze. I get up just to go to the bathroom, drink some water, eat a granola bar, and go back to bed. I'm so tired that I can't seem to do anything else. I sleep, and I sleep, and I sleep some more. Every time I get up, I find Aiden in the living room. Sometimes, he's eating. Other times, he's just watching television. Most of the time, he's either on his phone or on his laptop, furiously typing away.

And then, one day, I wake up and I'm no longer that

tired. Instead of heading straight out to the living room, I decide to take a shower. I climb in and let the warm water run over my body. I squeeze some shampoo into my palm and lather it into my hair. Then I wash it out and repeat the same thing with the conditioner. When I get out, I wrap myself in a towel and look in the mirror. The girl whose reflection looks back at me seems like a stranger. Is this the same person who only a few days ago walked barefoot on a sandy beach and imagined moving to that island with the love of her life? No, she's not. That girl was happy. That girl didn't abandon her best friend in the whole world to run away with her boyfriend.

I walk back to my room and put on a fresh shirt and a pair of pajama pants. I toss the ones that I've been living in for days on end into the laundry hamper and go out into the living room. Aiden is sitting at the dining room table with papers strewn all around him. His head is buried in his laptop and he doesn't even notice me until I walk past him and put on the kettle for some tea.

"Oh, hey!"

"Hey," I say. I walk over to him and give him a peck

on the cheek. "I'm going to make some breakfast. You want some?"

"No, I'm good," he says. "I actually ordered some pizza for dinner."

I glance at the clock. Oh, wow, it's 7:30 in the evening. I shrug and take out the eggs from the refrigerator. I scramble the eggs in a bowl, add some coconut milk, and cut up a piece of provolone cheese. I add some butter to the pan, watch as it sizzles, and pour the eggs. While they cook, I wash the fork and bowl in the sink under cold water.

"What are you working on?" I ask, swirling the eggs with a spatula until they're creamy.

"Just some work stuff."

"Okay."

When the eggs are done, I don't bother with a plate. Instead, I place the pan on the placemat at the other end of the table across from Aiden and dig in.

"Caroline's mom called," Aiden says after a moment. "The funeral is tomorrow."

"I'll be there," I say, nodding.

CHAPTER 15 - AIDEN

I want to be there for Ellie, but I don't know how. I see her suffering. For the first few days, all she did was sleep. She slept so much that I had to come into the room and actually check that she was still breathing to make sure that she was okay. She was. She has always been a big sleeper, but I've never seen anything like this. And now, she seems better. She's not sleeping anymore. She has showered. She washed her hair and changed her clothes. Even put on some makeup. But she's still not better. Somewhere behind that facade, Ellie is lost. And I don't know how to get her back.

I drive to the cemetery where they are going to have Caroline's funeral. Her mom organized the whole thing and had her assistant call to invite Ellie. It's about two hours away, near her parents' summer house in the Hamptons. Neither of us says anything for close to an hour. Ellie, because she doesn't want to, and me because I don't even know where to begin. Some topics seem too stupid to even approach. Others are too painful.

"This was one of Caroline's favorite places in the world," Ellie says. "She even told me that she wished she grew up here."

"The Hamptons?" I ask.

"Yep. She used to come here when she knew no one else would be here and just enjoy the place. Despite her big social life, she actually had a weakness for small town life. She often talked about how nice it would be to get a house and a small garden and chickens."

I nod. I find this hard to believe, given the person that I met, but who the hell really knows anyone? Ellie would of course know her better than I ever could.

"I like the Hamptons, too," I say, having nothing else to really add. I don't know if I should ask her more about Caroline or just let her bring it up herself. Maybe all she wants to do right now is to forget. Not forget about Caroline, but forget that this horrible thing ever happened to her best friend.

THE SERVICE IS cordial and respectful. Since everyone there is pretty much white, Anglo-Saxon, and Protestant, very few people shed any tears or express their emotions out loud. Ellie is having a hard time keeping her feelings at bay, but she squeezes my hand really hard from time to time and I whisper that it's all going to be okay.

"Thank you for coming, Ellie." Caroline's mom, Miriam, gives us both a quick hug. She's an attractive woman in her early fifties with a slim waist and big black sunglasses that make her look a lot like Jackie Kennedy. We both give her our condolences and tell her what a wonderful service this was. There isn't really much else to say in situations like these is there?

"What did the toxicology result say?" Ellie asks just as Miriam is about to walk away.

"Pardon me?"

Ellie repeats the question without batting an eye. I squeeze her arm, trying to convey that this might not be the most appropriate time for this conversation. But she doesn't really pay attention.

Miriam takes a deep breath. "They said it was an accidental overdose," she says. "She had a bunch of pills in her system. Oxy. Percocet. They said that she took a bit too much."

Accidental overdoses are a dime a dozen, especially with our generation of people. They happen all the time. I know of at least three people from high school who died from them. But knowing this isn't exactly going to make Ellie feel any better.

When Miriam walks away, Ellie walks away shaking her head.

"What's wrong?" I ask, keenly aware of how odd this question sounds at a funeral.

"Something's wrong. She didn't die of an accidental overdose."

"How do you know?"

Ellie shrugs and looks somewhere into the distance. "I don't know. I just do. She was always very careful with any sort of medication. She knew of a few people who overdosed and she never even mixed aspirin with booze."

"Well, she didn't say that she had any alcohol in her system," I say.

"I know. It just doesn't seem right."

"What are you saying, Ellie? That this wasn't an accident?"

"No," she says, shrugging. "I don't know."

On the drive home, I keep wondering what Ellie is thinking. If she doesn't think that this was an accidental overdose, there are really only two possible explanations. One is that it was on-purpose. And an on-purpose overdose is a suicide. That word sends shivers through my body. I look over at Ellie. Is this what she's thinking? That Caroline actually killed herself on purpose? I don't know Caroline well. Actually, I don't really know her at all. Does she have a history of depression? Is this something that she thought about before? I have no idea. She definitely didn't seem like a depressive. She was always excited and fun and ready to have a good time. But people are so much more complicated below the surface, aren't they?

The other possible explanation is that someone else did this to her. Someone put those drugs in her system. And that's what we would call murder. When Ellie found her, she was already cold. She did CPR, but she was dead for at least a few hours already. Whatever Ellie did for her was futile. Could someone else have been in their apartment before Ellie came home? Of course. Caroline had lots of friends. And she could've gone out and picked up some guy and brought him home. Perhaps it could've been a girl, but who the hell are we kidding? It's almost always a guy. But who would do this to her and why? I don't know Caroline well enough to even come close to coming up with some kind of motive. I want to ask Ellie about a million questions. When I look over, I see her leaning her head on the seat belt and aimlessly staring out of the window. Perhaps this isn't the best time.

After saying hello to her doorman, we head toward the elevator.

"Excuse me? Ms. Rhodes?" he calls out. Ellie turns around.

"This came today by courier," he says and hands her an envelope.

"Thank you," she says.

She tosses the letter on the kitchen island and heads to her room. A few days ago, Miriam came by with three movers and packed up all of Caroline's things. When Ellie saw what she was doing, she went to her room and stayed there until they left. Within a couple of hours, the whole room was stripped. They took everything. Down to the window treatments and the hooks that kept the paintings up on the walls. The place was left entirely barren. Miriam told me to tell Ellie that if she wants to live here for the rest of the lease, she's more than happy to pay for Caroline's part of the rent. She was just trying to be nice, but Ellie started to cry when I told her this bit. She hasn't been inside Caroline's room since then and hasn't even opened the door once.

My mind is spinning. I decide that the best thing for me to do at this junction is to just flip on the television and watch something stupid. The stupider the better. Grabbing a bag of chips from the pantry, I glance at the letter. Ellie usually gets all of her mail through the post office. Why was this one delivered by courier? Oh, shit, I hope it's not Blake's lawyers serving her with a lawsuit. That's the last thing she needs right now.

I pick up the envelope. When I read the return name and address, my heart skips a beat and all the blood drains from my face. It's from Caroline.

CHAPTER 16 - ELLIE

WHEN I READ THE LETTER...

Aiden bursts into my room without knocking and everything becomes a blur. He hands me a letter. He points to the name at the top. It's from Caroline. But how can that be? No, this isn't from my Caroline. This is all a terrible misunderstanding. A joke, even. A very unfunny and terrible joke.

"You have to read this. Please read this," Aiden says. I shake my head.

"I can't."

"Please, please open it. Caroline wanted you to."

I shake my head. I can't. I can't bear to know what it says.

"Can I open it?" he asks. I shrug. I guess. Why not?

"My dearest Ellie," Aiden reads. "If you are reading this letter, then I am in fact dead. I'm so, so sorry. I hate to do this to you because you are my closest friend, but there's no one else I trust. I'm sorry, Ellie, but I had to do it. My life was just not worth living anymore. Every night, I had nightmares over what Tom did to me. He haunted me all the time. He plagued me. No matter how many times I talked to the therapist about it, nothing made it better. But I know that this will. I know that this will put me out of my misery once and for all."

Tears start streaming down my face. Aiden stops reading, but I nudge him to continue.

"I love you, Ellie, and now I have to ask a favor. The biggest favor of my life. Please don't tell my parents about this letter. Please don't tell anyone, except maybe Aiden. For all I know, he's probably there with you anyway."

Aiden laughs. "She knows us too well," he says. I nod

and wipe my eyes, but more tears come to replace those that have just been wiped away.

"I did my best to make it look like an accidental overdose and that's what I want them to think. It's better this way. Less painful. I love you, Ellie. Forever and ever. I'm sorry I won't be able to share the rest of your life with you, but I just want you to know that you made my life bearable. And for that, I will be forever grateful. I'll see you again on this side or the other. Caroline."

Aiden takes me into his arms and I bury my face in his chest. Everything turns to black.

THE FOLLOWING MORNING, I wake up thinking that everything that just happened is a dream. Maybe I was just asleep for a very long time and none of it is real. When I climb out of bed, I see her letter on my desk. I run my fingers over it. No, unfortunately, this is not a dream. Not even a nightmare. Shit.

Suddenly, I hate her. What she did was beyond unfair. Who the hell does she think she is? Who gave her the right to do any of that? She kills herself and then covers it up? So, why tell me? Why do I have to be the only asshole out there who knows the truth? Why can't I just go on thinking that she had an accidental overdose just like her parents? Why do I have to have this burden to carry around with me?

I feel sick to my stomach. I barely make it to the toilet in time.

"Ellie? Are you okay?" Aiden yells from the other room. I hear him come into my bathroom and knock on the bathroom door.

"I'm fine," I mumble into the toilet bowl and throw up what's left of last night's meal. When I finally lift myself off the floor and brush my teeth, anger courses through my veins. I wash my face, but it doesn't make the fire that's building within me go away.

"Do you want me to make some breakfast?" Aiden asks.

"No thanks. I'm just going to have some tea."

I grab a seat at the island and stare into space.

"She planned this," I say. "She planned to kill herself."

"Yes."

"That letter was hand-delivered," I say, trying to understand her plan of action. I don't know why I feel the need to get to the bottom of what happened, but I do. "It wasn't mailed. Then it would've come too soon."

"Ellie—"

"If she would've mailed it, then it might've come without her being dead. No, she couldn't risk that. She had to have that letter be delivered after the funeral. The courier had to know for sure that she was dead."

"Ellie—"

Aiden keeps interrupting me, but I don't want to hear anything that he has to say.

"But I doubt that she told him what she was going to do. Maybe he just had to look for the announcement in the paper and then deliver the letter after he saw it."

"Ellie—"

"What?"

"Why are you doing this?"

"I don't know. Maybe it's because I'm a masochist, Aiden. I don't know."

Neither of us says anything for a while. My thoughts continue to swirl around what Ellie might have done to orchestrate this whole thing, but eventually they just settle on that little point in my chest where all the pain is focused.

"I just really miss her," I say, wiping the tears streaming down my cheeks.

"I know," Aiden says, putting his arm around me.

"What am I supposed to do now?"

"What do you mean?"

"With this letter? I feel like her family deserves to know the truth. But then again, I want to abide by her wishes."

"I don't know what to say."

"Why the hell did she have to put all of this on me? I mean, what the hell did I ever do to her?"

"You were her best friend, Ellie. She loved you. And

she knew that you loved her, too. That's why she left you the letter."

"Nice way of thanking me, huh?"

"She just wanted someone to know what really happened. Maybe she didn't want her last true act to be a lie."

Aiden is right. Of course, he's right. Caroline just wanted me to know that this wasn't an accident. That she went into that good night once and for all because she wanted to. Yet, the thought of that hurts even more than if it were an accident. I mean, the idea that my friend was in so much pain that she couldn't handle being alive anymore...how did I not realize this? Why didn't I see any of the signs? Oh, yes, of course. I was too busy with my own life. I was too obsessed with the idea of going on a wonderful vacation with the man of my dreams to pay any attention to those around me. I'm a terrible, horrible friend. Caroline deserved so much more than me.

"I don't think I'm going to tell anyone about this," I finally say, wiping my tears and pulling away from Aiden. "That's what Caroline would've wanted so that's what I'm going to do. I was a bad friend to her in life so I will try to be a better friend to her now that she's... gone."

Gone. This word is somehow more comforting than the alternative. Dead. My friend is dead. No, I'm not ready to say that out loud. Not yet. Perhaps never.

"You are a wonderful friend," Aiden says.

I shake my head. "Thank you, but no, I wasn't. I was a pretty bad friend."

"What's going to happen with the trial?"

"What?"

"The trial, in Maine? What's going to happen with that now?"

Oh my god. I completely forgot. All the blood drains from my face. Shit.

"Ellie, I'm so sorry, I didn't mean to bring it up," Aiden says. It's too late for that. Yes, of course. Caroline was the main witness against Tom. And now...what's going to happen now? Are they just going to let him go?

"They can still prosecute him without her, right?"

Aiden shrugs.

"Please tell me they can," I plead.

"I think so," he finally says. "But we are really going to have to talk to the district attorney."

I take a deep breath. My whole body starts to shake. Why the hell did you do this, Caroline? Why? You took your own life, but you had no right to. You are a selfish, narcissistic little girl. And I need you back. I can't live without you. How can the world continue existing without you in it? How can I?

CHAPTER 17 - AIDEN

I hang around Ellie's apartment and I try to make her better. I try, and I try, and I try and nothing works. I offer to make her food and I clean up, but it's all futile. There's nothing I can do to take the pain away. After a while I bury myself in work. I turn on my laptop and do what I do best.

It's not official yet, but I have my job back. It happened sometime during the fog of the last few weeks. The report that Ellie made against Blake became public knowledge and that was what pushed the Board of Directors to make the decision to ax him. Well, as soon as they did that, my attorneys reached out to them and made a suggestion. Since they didn't have any good options for Blake's replacement, why not go on the offensive and blame my firing on him. This isn't entirely untrue. In fact, it's probably ninety-nine percent true, so that's what they went with. Saving themselves some paper and effort, Owl's public relations team only had to put out one statement: firing him for allegations of sexual misconduct and hiring me back on a temporary basis.

But all of my good news is impossible to share at a time like this. Ellie is lost to the world. She's here, but not really here. Her body is present, but what about the rest of her? Where is she? I look at her staring out of the window. Her best friend is dead. And there's nothing I can do to fix it. I can't bring her back. I can't even say anything that would make it alright. And now, there's this damn letter. Why did Caroline have to leave that stupid letter? Why couldn't she just let Ellie go on believing that this whole thing was an accident? Why does Ellie have to be the only one who knows the truth?

When things get really tough, when I can't bear to watch her suffer all day and all night, I go into the office. I lie to her about where I'm going, even though she doesn't really ask, and I leave. The world outside continues to spin around the sun as if nothing has happened. It doesn't know anything about the sorrow that Ellie's experiencing inside her apartment, and maybe it's better for it.

After work, I wander the streets of New York to kill time. I stop by the library, check out a couple of books, and look through the romance section. I don't see any of Ellie's books there. Maybe they should be. She has so many people reading and buying her eBooks, why shouldn't she be stocked in the library as well? Unfortunately, this isn't a rhetorical question. I know the answer. Self-published books, no matter how good they are, don't get sold to libraries. At least, not very often. Libraries are mainly interested in buying traditionally published books because there's still a stigma against Indies. Ellie mentioned this earlier and I found out a lot more about this ever since. I would really like to give Ellie the gift of seeing her books in a real bookstore or library. Perhaps that can take her out of her funk.

I come back to Ellie's apartment with a heavy heart. This place is dreary and dark and full of bad memories. There are also good ones, but the black ones dominate right now. I want to go back to my place, but she refuses to come with me. She says she wants to be at home right now. Of course, I could go home by myself. But can I really do that? Should I? What if Ellie gets so sad that she also does something...irreversible? Until Caroline, I did not think this was possible. But now? Ellie is not herself. She's lost somewhere and until I get her back, I don't trust her on her own. I need to make sure that she's going to be okay.

"I picked up some Thai food," I say, placing all the takeout bags on the kitchen island.

"Okay," she yells from the bedroom. I wait for her to come out, but she doesn't.

"What are you doing?" I walk over. I find her sitting at her desk, staring out of the window.

"Nothing really. Just trying to write."

"How's it going?"

"Not well. It's all...blank. It just doesn't seem worth it anymore."

It's statements like these that really make me worry. Her writing has always been an escape for her. It has always been something that she absolutely had to do. Even before she wrote romance. I remember her telling me about writing her short stories and going over each word, sentence and paragraph with a fine-tooth comb. Her writing is the most definitive thing about her; it's the way that she relates to and understands the world.

"Maybe you should just take some time off, to clear your head," I suggest, but what the hell do I know about writing? Is time off even a good thing? Or does it just entrench you further in this pit of writer's block? The latter is typically the case when it comes to writing code - something I do know a thing or two about.

"Hey, come out and have some food," I say after she doesn't reply. "I want to tell you something."

Ellie grabs a seat across from me and picks up a spring roll. She stares at for a while and plays with it but doesn't take a bite.

"I should've told you this sooner, I know," I start. "But with everything that has been going on, I wasn't sure where to start."

"Okay."

"I sort of got my job back."

I watch her as she processes this statement. After a moment, her eyes light up.

"What do you mean?"

I give her the overview of what has been happening over the last few weeks. She puts the spring roll down as she listens. At the end, she gets out of her seat and wraps her arms tightly around my neck.

"Oh my God, are you serious?"

I nod. She kisses me on the lips. Tears run down her cheeks and she starts shaking uncontrollably. I pull her close to me and hold her until she stops.

"Are you okay?" I ask after a moment.

"Yes, of course! I'm more than okay," she says, wiping her tears. "I'm just so happy for you. So, is this for good?"

"I don't know yet. They fired Blake for good. And the board asked me to come back for a brief period of time as an interim CEO. Probably to keep the peace so to speak, to make sure that the investors don't start scrambling and the stock price doesn't continue to fall."

"That's great," she whispers, giving me another kiss.

"They say that they like my ideas, the ones that Blake rejected when he took over. And at least, they never really made it clear to the public why I left, they're now blaming it all on Blake to save some face."

"Well, it was pretty much his fault."

"Very true."

I'm honestly shocked by how well Ellie takes the news. I mean, I knew that she would be happy for me, but not this happy. I didn't think she would have much of a reaction.

"I'm actually sort of surprised by your reaction," I say as we both dig into the Thai food. "You have been in such a funk lately—"

"Yes, I know," Ellie says, finishing her spring roll and reaching for another. "And this news...I'm just so happy for you. Everything was just going to shit, you know. This really makes me feel better."

We enjoy the rest of our dinner over a few episodes of Friends on Netflix. I've only seen a few of them, but Ellie finds that unacceptable. According to her,

Friends is the type of show that will always improve your mood no matter how down in the dumps you are. A few hours later, right before we are about to turn in, Ellie's phone rings.

"I'm not going to answer it," she says. "I just want to get into bed and snuggle."

"I like the sound of that."

She brushes her teeth and her hair and climbs into bed next to me. I'm about to turn off the light when she reaches over me and looks at her phone.

"This is the DA from Maine," she says. "What could he have to say?"

I shrug and look at the time. It's after nine in the evening. Probably nothing good.

"It looks like he left a voice mail."

She puts it on speaker phone.

"Hi, Ellie, I'm sorry to call you so late. But I'm afraid I don't have very good news. I am going to have to drop the case against Tom Lackey since we no longer have Caroline's testimony. There may be a way to move forward if you are willing to be the star witness and your friend, Aiden Black, is also willing to testify, but I'm not sure. It's a long shot. Can you please give me a call back at your earliest convenience?"

"He's going to drop the case?" Ellie asks with tears welling up in her eyes. I shake my head.

"Not necessarily. Not if you and I testify on her behalf."

Ellie starts shaking and buries her head in her knees.

"He still said it was a long shot."

I put my arm around her shoulders and pull her close to me.

CHAPTER 18 - ELLIE

P eople say that time makes all pain duller and easier to deal with. I feel like it fills your life with so much darkness that at some point you just don't have space for any more of it. A week later, after I couldn't possibly cry anymore, I decide that I need to feel something else. I simply do not have the energy to mourn anymore. It wasn't that I was over anything. Not at all. I just have to feel another emotion if for no other reason than I have to see whether I am still capable of feeling other emotions.

I invite myself over to Aiden's for dinner. I open a bottle of wine and I ask him about his work. I'm so happy for him that he was able to get his job back. It's not official yet. It's just an interim position and there are no guarantees. Blake was the interim CEO before Aiden and look what happened to him. But it's better than nothing. It's a shot. And that's all Aiden needs right now. Owl is his baby. It was something he grew, cultivated, and cared for his whole adult life. Losing it had made a hole in his heart that would've taken years to fill. And now? Well, things are looking up.

"So, what do you want to do tonight? Binge on some Netflix?" Aiden asks me, helping me clear the table.

"Something like that," I say with a wink.

Aiden raises his eyebrows in surprise.

"I was thinking more like Netflix and chill."

"Oh, really?" he asks, nearly dropping one of the plates.

"Don't act so shocked."

"I'm not."

I walk over to him and take his hand. I lead him to the bedroom. After sitting him down on the bed, I pull out the piece of paper that I found in his office.

"This is the contract that you asked me to sign," I say, handing it to him. "I've signed it."

Aiden looks at the contract, at me, and back at the contract.

"Tonight, I'm yours to do with as you please."

"Ellie, I don't want you to feel like you owe me something. I totally understand what you're going through."

"No, it's not about that."

"So what? What is this about?"

"I'm just really tired of feeling so shitty. And I need to feel something else. Will you make me feel something else...Mr. Black?"

MR. BLACK GETS a coy smile on his face. He walks over to the nightstand and gets out a pair of handcuffs. Wow, that was quick. He leads me to the desk. I'm wearing a thin dress with spaghetti straps and he slowly pushes the straps off my shoulders. My whole body shudders. My nipples get hard and a familiar warm sensation starts to build within my body. I press my legs together, but he pushes them apart with his knees.

"Oh, no," Mr. Black says, shaking his head. With one swift motion, my dress falls to the floor and I'm standing in nothing but a bra and panties. He unclasps my bra and lets my breasts fall into his hands.

"Oh, wow," I whisper as he kneels down and takes my nipple into his mouth. He massages my other breast with his hand and then switches sides. My panties are getting wetter and wetter with each passing second. Just when they are pretty much soaked, Mr. Black pulls them down.

"Wow, that was fast," I say. He shrugs and pushes me down to the floor. Then he pulls my arms up and handcuffs them above my head. Each motion is swift and direct. He's in control and there's nothing I can do about it. At least there's nothing I really want to do, except to let him take me on this wild ride.

After pushing my legs apart, he gets down on the

floor in front of me and spreads my legs. Then he buries his head in between them. This time, however, his motions are no longer swift or fast. No, now he takes his time. He lets his warm tongue run over every part of me prior to burying itself deep inside. He swirls it around and around until my head starts to spin and I forget about everything else in the world. Suddenly, the outside world ceases to exist entirely

"Wow, that feels so good," I mumble and slump back against the leg of the desk. Luckily, it's rounded and only slightly digs into my back.

"I'm getting close," I whisper as he starts to make concentric circles with his tongue.

"Oh, no, we can't have that."

He pulls himself away from me and unlocks my handcuffs. I expect him to take me over to the bed, but he simply turns me around to face the desk and places me on all fours. Then he handcuffs me to the leg of the desk again. My butt is now facing him. I'm stark naked and entirely exposed and it never felt so good.

He spreads my legs with his hands and pushes his

finger deep within me. I moan in pleasure and say his name.

"Aiden? Who's Aiden?" he asks, plunging his fingers deeper within me, making me moan even louder in pleasure.

"Mr. Black," I correct myself.

"That's better."

While some of his fingers continue to swirl within me, others make their way toward my clit. They massage it and play with it, but stop short every time I feel like I'm about to reach my climax.

"You're toying with me," I whisper.

"Of course."

I hear the ruffling of his clothes somewhere behind me. Before I get the chance to look back, I feel his big powerful cock plunge within me. He pierces me and then slides in and out, spreading me further apart.

"Oh, that feels so good."

"It better," Mr. Black says. His legs are in between mine, plunging in and out of me. He pulls his fingers away from my clit and stands up straight, holding me by my hips. He uses my hips as his guide, but quickly this isn't enough for him. Oh, no. Before I know it, he makes his way toward my ass. At first, he squeezes each of my ass cheeks and then he presses his fingers inside of me. As he continues to slide and out of me, my whole body starts to tingle.

"Come for me," Mr. Black commands. I take a deep breath and let go. Finally. Every part of my body explodes in pleasure as I let out one big moan. My head starts to spin and all I see around are stars before everything fades to black. A moment later, I hear Aiden yell out my name from behind me and fall down on top of me.

Drenched in sweat, we lie here in silence for a few moments before he says, "that was so good."

"Yes, that was kind of amazing," I mumble. "I love you, Aiden, and I love Mr. Black."

"I'm glad you do."

He unlocks my handcuffs and I snuggle up to him. He wraps his arms around me and we lie here, lost to the world outside.

"I want to stay here forever," I say.

"Me, too."

"I'm really sorry about everything."

"What are you talking about?"

"I've just been so cold to you. Not just that. I've been so lost. I don't know," I say.

"You've been mourning your best friend, Ellie. I totally understand."

I let out a sigh and it feels like the weight of the world lifts off my shoulders.

"I should've never broken off our engagement," I say after a moment. "I want to marry you. I want to be with you."

Aiden leans over and kisses me on the lips. "I want to marry you, too. But I don't want to rush into anything. I'm here for you. I'm yours. And I will marry you the minute that you say you want to. But I will stay with you forever even if you never want to."

This statement makes me want to marry him even more. But he's right. I'm just lost in the moment. Overcome with emotion. Overcome with feelings of...anything. Actually, this is the first time that I felt like someone who wasn't grieving. This is the first time that I forgot about what just happened and enjoyed myself. I need to savor this. I need this to last.

CHAPTER 19 - ELLIE

The following morning is the first time I feel somewhat normal. I faintly remember Aiden giving me a kiss on the cheek and telling me that he has to go to work, but that was hours ago. Now, it's way past ten. I stretch and slowly get out of bed. The sun is shining and birds are singing outside. I climb into the shower and enjoy the way the hot water runs down my body. For a few minutes there, I feel okay. Actually, more than okay. My thoughts go back to last night and a warm sensation starts to pool in between my legs. Okay, okay. You need to calm down, I say to myself. You can't get aroused again. At least, not yet. You have all that work to catch up on.

After getting out of the shower, I sit down at his desk and check my emails. I've been browsing through them every day, but to say that I was actually checking them would be a bold-faced lie. When I check my email this morning, I have over two-hundred unopened ones and another hundred or so which I've read but still need replies. This is just too big of a problem to tackle right now. No, I can't do this. Instead, I turn my attention to the latest installment of my Auction series. I was about a third of the way through it before that happened. I carefully review my notes to try to figure out where I was in the writing process. Much to my surprise, I discover that I was in the middle of a very exciting chapter.

I can do this, I decide. I jot down a few notes of where I want the story to go and then set the timer. I always write in twenty minute intervals. I start the time on my phone and then write according to the outline that I wrote down. Sometimes, I stick to it. Other times, I go off script. The characters talk to me and become their own people and I let them. I don't constrain them, I let them go. It's when I decided to let them be free, and become the people that they are meant to be, that my writing got so much better than it ever was before.

When I start to type, the words just flow out of me and the twenty minutes expire in what seems like only five minutes. The timer goes off when I'm in the middle of a scene, so I press return a few times to continue the sentence a little further down the page and get back to work. The next twenty minutes flies by just as fast as the first and I'm still not done. I haven't written in a long time and the words just keep pouring out of me. I guess last night's escapades invigorated me much more than I had previously thought. When the timer goes off for the third time, I decide to take a break. I count up the words that each session produced. Seven hundred fifty, eight hundred sixty-seven, and nine hundred ninety-eight. That's a total of two thousand six hundred and fifteen words. Not bad. Not bad at all.

Perhaps, I should keep this streak going. I pick up a pen and start to write down my ideas for the next scene. But then...oh, no. I press my hand to my stomach. Oh my God. No, no, no.

I run to the bathroom. Luckily, the lid to the toilet is already open because I wouldn't be able to make it otherwise. Before I'm even able to kneel down, I start vomiting. I puke until I can't puke anymore, and when it feels like I've flushed all of my insides down the toilet, then I puke some more.

"Oh my God," I whisper, wiping the tears running down my cheeks. I'm not crying, they just come with the process. Somewhere in between the gags, my thoughts turn back to Caroline. I haven't thought of her this whole morning. This was the first morning in weeks that was, by all accounts, normal. And now, suddenly, it's not. I'm throwing up and I have no idea why. It has something to do with Caroline. I haven't thought about her for some time and now I have to make amends. This is my punishment for forgetting her.

I barf again. And again. In between, I lie down on the tile floor and try to cool off. I'm not particularly cold. But I am covered in sweat. My entire body is out of whack. One minute my teeth are chattering and the next I'm perspiring as if I had just gone on a two mile hike through the Mohave Desert in the middle of summer. What the hell is going on? This can't all have to do with Caroline, can it? No, maybe I ate something bad. I try to think. The last time I ate anything was last night. But then I would've gotten sick last night, right? Isn't that how stomach flu works? I don't actually know. I very rarely get sick and I hardly ever throw up.

I drape myself over the toilet and wait for more to come. But this time, it doesn't. I flush the toilet and stare at the water as it fills up the bowl. Gathering some strength, I pull myself up to my feet and wash my face in the sink. The shakes have subsided a bit, but I still feel like I'm freezing. I change out of the sweat-drenched clothes and climb into bed. No, this has to do with Caroline. I threw up when I first learned about her death and here I am throwing up now as well. Is this how it's going to be now? I'm going to go hours without thinking about her and then have this violent reaction at the end? Is this my way of not forgetting her?

CHAPTER 20 - ELLIE

WHEN I STILL DON'T FEEL WELL…

I stay in bed most of the afternoon with occasional trips to the toilet. The only thing that seems to settle my stomach is bread. I can't even drink very much water because it also makes me violently sick and sends me running toward the bathroom. Even standing upright makes my head spin.

"I stopped by and got some chicken broth," Aiden says when he comes over after work. I hate him seeing me like this. Sick like a dog. Dressed in nothing but sweats with a smidge of makeup in sight.

"Thank you, but you really shouldn't have."

"Hey, I'm going to nurse you back to health if it's the last thing I do."

"You're too sweet," I say. And he's true to his word. He waits on me all evening, bringing me chicken broth and making me toast upon request. He even climbs into bed with me, when I explicitly tell him not to, so we can watch Netflix.

"I don't want you to get sick," I say. "I mean, I might have a bad strain of the flu or something. You really should go home."

"You're throwing up every hour, Ellie. I'm not going home."

I shrug and snuggle up to him tighter. I don't have the energy to fight with him now.

"You know, this is the first time either one of us has ever been ill," I say after a while.

"Yeah, I guess."

"Well, isn't it a saying that you really shouldn't decide whether the guy or girl you're seeing is a keeper until the first time you're sick?"

"Why is that?" he asks.

"Because it's all about whether that person is there for you. You're not looking your best and you're going through something pretty rough, and it's all about whether or not the other person shows up and cares for you."

"And how am I doing?" he asks, giving me a squeeze.

"Very well. You're doing an excellent job, actually. So good in fact that you've earned bonus points and you should probably go home now."

"No way," Aiden says definitively.

In this moment, I know that I will never love anyone as much I love him.

THE FOLLOWING MORNING, I wake up as sick as the previous one. I spend close to an hour draped over the toilet. I'm so ill in fact that Aiden actually decides to work from home. He brings me tea, crackers, and toast and refuses go in to work no matter how much I beg him to. In the afternoon, I feel good enough to actually come out to the living room and watch television there. Aiden talks on the phone and types furiously on his laptop until five o'clock when he turns everything off and joins me on the couch. Our takeout arrives fifteen minutes after. I wasn't sure what to order so Aiden ordered a variety of different Vietnamese dishes and appetizers just in case some things didn't sit well with me.

"I have to tell you something," Aiden says after I manage to eat one pot sticker. "This may not be the best time, but I just can't wait any longer. I know that I should've told you this sooner."

"Okay," I say. For a second, I think it might be something romantic, but by the look on his face, it's probably something serious. Damn. I'm really not in the mood for anything like that.

"I talked to the DA. From Maine? About Caroline's case," Aiden says as if I don't know who he's referring to.

"About what?"

"She was going to drop the case, Ellie. Without Caroline pressing charges and testifying, they were going to let Tom go."

"So, it's over?" I feel like someone has just punched me in the throat.

"Well, here's the thing. The case that she had against him technically is over. But that's not the only thing they have on him."

My head is starting to buzz and I start to feel sick again. I can't really hear or process anything that he's saying. Even though Aiden is sitting right next to me, it feels like we're talking to each other from across a football field.

"I don't understand," I say.

"I told her, Ellie. I told her that Caroline didn't overdose by accident. I told her that she committed suicide. And that you have proof."

"You told her what??" I try to get up and my head starts to swim again. "I can't believe you! You totally betrayed my trust."

"I'm sorry, Ellie, but she was going to let Tom go. He was going to get off. I just couldn't let that happen."

I shake my head. "Who the hell do you think you are, Aiden? Caroline trusted me. She didn't want anyone to know."

"But I'm not sure she knew that her suicide would mean that Tom would get off the hook. I don't think she thought of all the consequences."

"And if she did?"

"I don't know. I just thought this was the right thing to do."

"Well, it wasn't!" I yell. I've never really yelled at Aiden like this before. I've never really been this angry at him before.

"Well, the DA thinks that she might have a case now. She wants to see the letter. She wants us both to testify at the trial. She's going to build a case against Tom, saying that he caused her suicide."

"I don't care, Aiden. That letter— she left that letter to me. I was supposed to protect her secret. She trusted me."

I'm just repeating myself over and over because it's all I can do. A million thoughts run through my head and I can't stop any of them. I can't even slow them down.

Aiden keeps trying to explain. He did this because he didn't want me to be the one who broke my promise to Caroline. It's not really breaking a promise if he did it. Caroline didn't really understand what she was doing. But none of these arguments make any sense. Maybe I just don't want them to. No, right now, I just want one thing.

"I want you to leave," I finally say.

"What?"

I repeat myself. He protests and says that I shouldn't be alone when I'm feeling so badly, but I insist.

"I need you to leave. Now," I say as firmly as I can. I'm in no mood to talk anymore. I need time to think this over. Time away from him.

My stomach starts to grumble again. I take one deep breath after another, hoping I can keep the nausea at bay until he leaves. A few minutes later, Aiden is finally gone.

I get up and run to the bathroom.

CHAPTER 21 - ELLIE

WHEN I STILL DON'T FEEL WELL...

My anger with what Aiden did intensifies throughout the night. I'm angry at him for going behind my back. I'm angry at him for revealing Caroline's secret. I'm angry that now her mother will likely find out the truth and that's not what Caroline wanted. But I'm also angry at him because I know deep down that he might have done the right thing. A predator like Tom should not get away with what he did just because he did something so horrible that Caroline actually killed herself over it. He shouldn't be allowed to walk the streets because of a technicality. I saw him. He's not one bit sorry or apologetic. And the DA dropping charges against him would just make him more cocky and righteous. No, Tom needs to pay for this. But it should've been my decision. I was the one who should've gone to her and told her about Caroline's letter. But then again, if I had done that then I would've been the one breaking my promise to her.

I can't sleep. I get up and pace around the apartment. When I get a drink of water in the kitchen, my eyes meander over the calendar. What date is it? Hmm. That's odd. Wait a second. When was the last time that I had my period? My heart skips a beat as I try to remember. Not last week or the previous week. But four weeks ago, yes. I did have my period then. Okay. That's a relief.

At least I'm not pregnant, I say to myself as I plop on the couch and flip on the television. I lie down and zone out for a while, watching late night re-runs of King of Queens. When I wake up an hour later, I again feel sick to my stomach. Perfect. I guess this is just a really bad case of the flu.

I pull myself off the couch, about to head back to my bathroom. But the nausea feeling overwhelms me and I run into the bathroom in the hallway instead. This was technically Caroline's bathroom, but it was also the one that guests used when they came over. As I throw up, it occurs to me that I haven't been in here since Caroline died. This realization makes me even more sick to my stomach. Afterward, sitting on the closed toilet, I look under the sink. It's filled with all the things that Caroline used that her mom didn't take with her. Caroline's hairdryer. Extra hand soap and shampoo and conditioner. Her scale. And there in the back is the unopened box with two pregnancy tests.

I open the box and take one out. I don't need to read the instructions. I've taken one before in college. It showed what my period confirmed later that day that I wasn't pregnant.

This is so stupid, I say to myself. There's no way I'm pregnant. I just have some stupid stomach flu. People get them all the time.

But why not take it anyway? They're here. Available. If it's not a big deal, then why not do it?

I take a deep breath.

"Okay, if you're going to do it, do it now before you have to throw up again," I say. I open the package and pull down my panties. After I pee on the stick, I turn back around and get sick again. It takes a few minutes for the test to show the results and I wait lying on my back on the cold tiles. Then I reach up for the test and look at the screen.

"Pregnant."

CHAPTER 22 - AIDEN

I leave Ellie's apartment fuming. How does she not understand that I was just trying to help her? It's not like I wanted to reveal Caroline's secret. But it's something that had to be done. Besides, if Caroline didn't want anyone to know that she actually killed herself, why did she leave a note? No, she wanted everyone to know the truth. Maybe she didn't want her mom to know, but she wanted someone to know. She wanted Ellie to know. She probably wanted Tom to know as well. He's the one who is largely responsible for her suicide. He was the one who violated her. Killing herself was her way of not dealing with the pain he'd caused her any longer. Fuck, it just breaks my heart that she did this.

It also makes me want to kill Tom. Or at the very least, beat the daylights out of him.

It starts to rain. I pull the collar of my jacket tighter around my neck to keep some of the chill away from me. Unfortunately, it does fuck all. Taking a walk in the fresh air seemed like a good idea only ten minutes earlier, but now I willfully regret the decision. As much as I try to put everything that just happened at Ellie's out of my mind, my thoughts just keep drifting back. How can she not understand? The reason that I talked to the District Attorney is that I didn't want Caroline's death to be in vain. I didn't want an asshole like Tom walking the streets among us. He needs to be punished for what he did. Or at the very least, people need to learn the truth about him. If I just let the letter go and bury it along with Caroline, Tom stays out there in the world, free to do something like this to another woman. No, I couldn't have that. The main witness against Tom is no longer available to testify against him. So, without the letter, the DA would have no choice but to drop the case. And now? Well, now there's at least hope.

I walk the last few blocks with my head in the clouds. Everything that made perfect sense just a few hours ago, no longer makes any sense at all. The cold air, which is supposed to clear my head, just makes it all that much worse. I clench my fists. Anger is building up deep within me, the kind that burns slowly, and the kind that I don't really know how to deal with at all. And the worst thing? It's directed at Ellie. I'm angry with her. Mostly angry, but also disappointed. Why is she being so obtuse? Is it deliberate? Why can't she meet me halfway on this? How dare she kick me out? Just as things were starting to look up.

Perhaps I'm not cut out for relationships. Or at least this one. Should things really be this hard? I mean, we haven't been dating that long. And we've already endured all of this drama. No, it's just too hard.

"Hey!" someone yells as I turn the corner. My building is within view, at the end of the block, and I'm not in the mood to make small talk with some stranger.

"Hey!" the guy says again. Against my better judgement, I turn around. A gale force wind slams into my face. I put my hand up to block some of the wind and rain so I can see who's trying to get my attention.

"You're such an asshole, you know that, Aiden?" the guy says, stepping out of the shadow.

"What are you doing here, Blake?" I ask. He takes a step back. His footing is uneasy and he nearly falls, catching himself on the wall.

"Hey!" he says again, slurring his words. As he leans closer to me, a strong odor of alcohol slams into my face.

"Go home. You're drunk."

"I will not go...home."

"Fine," I say, turning away from him. "I am."

Just as I'm about to walk away, he grabs my shoulder.

"Where are you going?" he asks. "You think you can get me fired and then...then what? Just go away?"

I shrug him off, but he refuses to let me go. Instead, he grabs me by my neck and presses my face toward his.

"You...got me...fired, you ass...hole," he mumbles.

I grab his hands and peel him away from me. Once I free my neck, I give him a strong shove. He

bounces back a few steps and braces himself
against the wall.

"I'm not going to talk about this right now," I say.
"You're drunk. If you want to discuss this later, give
me a call."

"Fine, I...will," he says. "Don't think I won't."

This time I don't wait for him to grab onto me again.
I turn up my collar and walk toward my building.
Anger, which has been growing within me, bubbles
toward the surface. But it's no longer aimed at Ellie.
No, my anger is directed entirely at Blake. Who does
he think he is? Why the fuck is he stalking me?
Showing up near my house? All the shit that he did
to Ellie and to me...and he's blaming me? All I see
is red.

A few minutes later, I get home and pour myself a
glass of whiskey. As the dark, soothing liquid runs
down my throat, I start to feel a little better. My
anger dissipates a little bit and is quickly replaced
with just a general feeling of loss and
disappointment. There was a time, not that long ago,
when Blake was a friend. And not just a friend, a
really close friend. My best friend. We have been

friends since Yale. He was the one person who was there with me when I started Owl, my company. He was there through its meteoric rise. And yet, he was the one who was largely responsible for my downfall. In fact, he was the instrumental actor who caused my downfall. But why? During all that time that I thought we were close friends, did he secretly hate me?

The intercom rings. When I answer, the doorman says that it's Blake Garrison here to see me.

"Don't let him up," I say. I'm about to hang up, when I hear some commotion on the other end.

"You asshole! You think you can just take my job?" Blake yells into the phone. He must've grabbed it away from the doorman. "You're going to pay for this! You and your slut girlfriend. You're both going to be sorry when I'm through with you!"

CHAPTER 23 - ELLIE

This can't be real. Pregnant? Me. I look down at the test. This isn't one of those one line or two line tests. What happens if one of them is faint? No, this test is pretty clear. The words appear in black and white.

Pregnant.

Pregnant!

Fucking pregnant!!!

I can't breathe. My muscles seize up and no air comes in or out of my throat. A moment later, I start to cough. Little ripples thrust through my whole body, shaking me uncontrollably. Just when I think it's over with, and I can finally catch my breath, I feel it come on again. The vomit. I lean over the toilet and spit out what is left of my insides.

This can't be real. No, no, no. How can this happen? We were so careful. I am on the pill and I've been taking it religiously. It's about the only thing I've been doing religiously. After brushing my teeth for what feels like the millionth time, I head into the kitchen and open the refrigerator. I feel like I want to eat something, but nothing looks good, or even mildly appetizing. No, it's all so... gross. Somewhere in the back of the cupboard next to the stove, that Caroline and I referred to as our pantry, I find an opened pack of dry saltine crackers. Caroline, who has always been terrified of carbohydrates, as if they were poison, kept these stashed away in the back in case of emergencies. Alcohol poisoning, dry heaving, unable to get off the bathroom floor type of emergencies.

As I pop one in my mouth, tears start to stream down my face. Suddenly, I miss Caroline more than I ever missed anyone before. I want to see her. I need to talk to her. I don't really have any other friends. She's the only person I can really talk to about this. And Aiden? No, I'm not ready for that.

"Caroline," I say out loud. My voice is slow and unsteady. I've never talked to a dead person before, but it feels good just to say her name again. "Caroline, I'm so, so sorry. I should've been here for you. I should've stuck around not just run off to the Caribbean with my boyfriend. I knew that you needed help and I just didn't care."

That's not entirely true, of course. If Caroline would've told me how she felt or acted more out of it, I would've never gone. But she didn't. She pretended to be fine. She acted as if everything was okay.

"You should've gone with me. I knew you wanted to. And we could've taken you out of your head. Then, maybe...you'd still be here."

I wait for her to answer even though I know that I won't hear anything. After a few minutes, I continue.

"And now? What the hell am I supposed to do now, Caroline? The test says I'm pregnant. But...that can't be. I'm too young. I'm not ready. Aiden and I...well, I love him but that doesn't mean I want to have a kid with him."

I pace around the room aimlessly. Now, I'm no longer waiting for a response. No. Now, I'm just ranting out loud like a crazy person. But just putting my thoughts into words is making me feel a little better.

"Why the hell are you not here, Caroline? I need you. I need you to tell me what to do. And if not that, just to listen to me. I don't know what to do, Caroline." I break down and slump to the floor. Tears stream down my cheeks. "I don't know what to do."

I'm no longer able to speak. My voice cracks and disappears entirely. I wrap my arms around my knees and lie down in a fetal position and just cry until no more tears come. I cry for my best friend. I cry for myself. I cry for the unborn baby that I'm carrying within me. And at the end, I cry for Aiden. I don't know what he will say, or do, in response to this, and I don't want to find out.

I stay on the floor until I lose all sense of time. Seconds become minutes and then probably hours. The texture of the light that streams through my window changes, but I don't recognize it as either morning, afternoon, evening, or night. And just as everything seems far away and lost forever, I turn over. My shoulders hurt from lying on the cold hard floor as I prop myself up with my hands and sit up.

"Okay, Ellie. You can do this," I say to myself. I don't really believe it, but then I manage to stand up.

Good job. Now, walk over to kitchen counter and make yourself some tea. Unlike a stream of consciousness, in which you barely acknowledge each word but just do things on instinct, these thoughts are completely different. They are actual, deliberate sentences with carefully chosen words. I have to say them to myself, otherwise, I couldn't do it.

The water in the kettle boils and I dunk an herbal tea bag a few times, watching it as it first floats to the surface and then slowly sinks to the bottom of the cup. The hot water feels soothing going down my throat, and it helps me to focus. Right now, the problem is not that I have too many thoughts running through my mind, but actually the opposite. My mind is completely blank. It's as if my brain is entirely empty and I need to think just to fill it with something, anything.

Before I go freaking out about the results of this pregnancy test, I need to make sure that I'm actually pregnant. Drug store tests are notorious for their false positives. Right? I heard that somewhere once. So, before I start imagining all sorts of eventualities and possible outcomes and decisions that I might have to make, I have to first make sure that this is accurate. Verifiable. True. And I have to get this confirmation before I tell Aiden. Because, as of right now, there's nothing really to tell.

CHAPTER 24 - ELLIE

WHEN I HAVE TO GO THERE…

I've never been to see a gynecologist before. It's kind of pathetic, I know. But as I sit here in this little office with no ventilation, I realize that this is actually quite true. The thing is that I hate doctors. I've always hated going to see doctors since I was little, and dentists, so when I came of age, I just never went. Some girls have been going since they were in their teens, to get prescriptions for birth control pills, but I just bought it from a friend. It seemed so much easier that way. Frankly, I don't even know why they force you to see a doctor before giving a prescription for birth control pills. I mean, c'mon. Condoms can be bought just about anywhere, so why not pills?

Of course, I'm terribly embarrassed over this whole thing. It's not something anyone knows, except for Caroline of course. And she took this info to the grave with her. The other thing that I really hate about doctors' offices is that I have to deal with all of this insurance crap just to get in. It's not enough to just look up a list of doctors online in a particular specialty and read their reviews to see if it's someone I want to see. No, I also have to check if they are in my network and how much I would have to pay for a co-pay. I already pay $500 a month for my health insurance, but in addition to that, I also have to pay a $70 copay for the visit. As soon as I arrived, they gave me a clipboard with four pages of questions to answer about my health history. Of course, there was that all frightening *when was the date of your last period?* Question, which I never have a good answer for and today is no exception. For some reason, this question appeared on every form that I filled out at Yale's health clinic - the last place where I saw a physician, even when I just went in with a cold in search for a prescription for some strong antibiotics.

I browse through the magazines as I wait to be called. There are two other women who are waiting with me. One is visibly pregnant and another is trying to get her fussy baby to sleep. Fussy. Now, there's a word. A particularly kind word actually. A more accurate description of this baby, however, would be screaming. Angry. Incredibly upset. The woman looks frazzled. Her hair is disheveled and she is without a smidge of makeup. She is dressed in sweats and there's spit up or throw up or some other white substance near her shoulders. I glance over at the pregnant woman. She is staring at the new mother and looks terrified. After a few minutes, she asks her how old her baby is and comments on how cute it is. Frankly, it doesn't look particularly cute to me, but what the hell do I know? I bury my nose in the latest issue of Oprah magazine, which talks about setting goals for your dreams to make them a reality.

Dreams. Now, there's a far off concept. Not long ago, my dream was to become a writer. All I wanted was for people to read my stories and enjoy them. Making a little bit of money off them would've been a perk. But getting married? Having a kid? Buying a house in the suburbs? Something tells me that this is not the kind of dream that the O Magazine article is referring to. No, these kinds of things are just mundane, run of the mill things that happen to everyone right? Or most people, I guess. Perhaps, there are people out there who dream of these things. But me? No, thank you. That's not what I want. At least, not right now. No, that's the last thing I want, actually. What I really want is to see my books on top of the charts. I want more and more people buying them. I want to get them into bookstores and to see them on shelves. I want to be interviewed on TV about them. I want to be written up in O Magazine as a recommended read.

Fucking hell. I put the magazine up to my face so that the two women in the waiting room don't see me, in case I start crying. What the hell am I doing here? I can't be pregnant. And even if I am, I don't want this baby. This is the last thing I want. I don't want to spend my days and nights taking care of some other human being. Some helpless, completely dependent, incompetent person who can't even hold up his or her head. No, thank you. That kind of life isn't for me.

"Ellie Rhodes?" A woman with a clipboard opens the door to the waiting room and invites me to the back. My heart is racing and I feel like I'm about to hyperventilate. Then I feel sick to my stomach.

"I think I'm going to throw up," I say.

"The bathroom is right through there. When you're done, please write your name on the paper cup and pee in it. Then place it on the pass through window ledge. We will need to confirm whether you are, or are not, pregnant."

I barely finish listening to her instructions before I disappear into the bathroom. After I throw up, yet again, I do as she says. I place my cup on the ledge, wash my hands, and walk outside.

CHAPTER 25 - ELLIE

WHEN I GET HELP...

I leave the gynecologist's office in a daze, her words still ringing in my ears. I feel like I'm both floating on air and being chained to the ground by some invisible force. I head straight to the pharmacy at the end of the corner. Do I need to get a confirmation of a confirmation? How accurate is the pregnancy test at the doctor's office, anyway?

Just then a new wave of nausea comes over me. I bend over a trashcan and dry heave for a few minutes. A few people slow down when walking past me, but no one stops. This is New York at its best. I actually don't mind. If I weren't so sick, I'd be mortified. But right now, nothing else comes to mind except for what is the fastest way that I can get home so that I can lie down. After all of this throwing up, I finally come to the realization that what makes the nausea that much worse is actually being physically upright.

The fastest way home is to hail a cab or grab a Lyft. Then I'd be there in five minutes. But I can't go home directly. I got a prescription for an anti-nausea pill from the doctor and I need to fill it. I need something to make all of this pain go away. It's giving me a splitting headache. And I need a clear head to think.

I barely manage to drag myself a block over to the nearest Rite Aid. Walking past the makeup aisle, I glance at myself in the mirror near the lipsticks. Holy fuck. What a sight! My hair is sticking out in all directions - the messy bun is so messy that it's way beyond being cool. It's not even in the same ballpark as cool. My skin is splotchy and pale. My lips are chapped and peeling and I have big black bags under my eyes.

It's the middle of the day, so there's no wait at the pharmacy counter. I tell the woman in a white coat my name and that my doctor called in a prescription for Diclegis. She takes my insurance card and walks to the back. A few moments later, she comes back.

"Actually, your insurance doesn't cover this."

"What?"

She repeats herself.

"But my doctor said this was the best. This will make me feel better."

"The way that your insurance will cover this is if you first try Zofran. This is a new medication so you need special approval."

"Okay," I say. I have no idea how to deal with this situation.

"The problem is that your doctor didn't call in a prescription for Zofran. Just Diclegis."

"Shit," I mumble.

"You could give them a call and ask them to prescribe Zofran for you first. Then you can try it and if it doesn't work, you can come in for Diclegis. Or you can pay for Diclegis out of pocket."

I inhale deeply. My nausea is coming back with a vengeance.

"Please step aside, ma'am," she says. "May I help you?"

There's a line forming behind me. I can't make this decision here right now. Shit. I dial the doctor's number and wait on the line. In the meantime, I look up both medications online. Diclegis definitely seems safer. It's just an antihistamine, an over the counter sleeping pill, and vitamin B6 with a slow release formulation to make sure that it stays in your system for longer. Zofran, on the other hand, well, there are people noting that it might be responsible for some birth defects.

"How much is the Diclegis if I just buy it now?" I ask, after I wait in line for my turn.

"You want to buy out of pocket?"

"Yes. I mean, maybe. I mean, I have a prescription right?"

The woman nods and shakes her head. Then she rings up my prescription.

"$750."

"What?"

She repeats the preposterous number.

"But both of its components are available over the counter. Why the hell is it so expensive?"

"This is America, ma'am," the woman says in the most deadpan voice ever.

"Okay, fine," I say. "I'll take it."

"Are you sure?"

I shrug. "No one is answering at the doctor's office and I feel like I'm going to die. So, I'll figure this out when I'm feeling better."

I hand her my credit card and she rings me up. Signing the bottom, I suddenly realize how lucky I am that money isn't a problem. These stupid pills are $750, and that's a ton of money by anyone's standards. And yet, here I am, willing to pay for it out of pocket just so I can go home and not throw up so much.

On the way out, I grab a bottle of water, a bag of

potato chips, which look mildly appetizing, some sour candy, and a bottle each of Unisom (the over the counter antihistamine) and B6. Maybe I can see if taking the combination of these two meds will help me on their own and I won't need Diclegis at all. But I'll have it as a backup. As I wait to be checked out the second time, I feel sick again and throw up a little into a plastic bag that I grab from the counter at the very last minute.

I DIDN'T BOTHER WAITING to get home to take the B6 pills and the Unisom. I read the instructions for combining the two on my phone while waiting in line and hope to God that it works by the time I get home. Unfortunately, I'm not so lucky. The nausea just gets worse and worse and three hours later, I'm convinced that my over the counter solution isn't doing me any good. So, I grab the bag of Diclegis and pop two pills into my mouth. I lie back down in bed, put Friends on Netflix and wait for the room to stop spinning.

I don't know how many hours pass as I wait, but eventually it does, somewhat. Netflix asks me if I am still wanting to continue my binge a few times at least, and the afternoon sun has long since disappeared into the Hudson River. The next time I have to get out of bed, it's pitch black outside and I have to turn on the light just to make it to the bathroom. Much to my surprise, however, I don't feel that dizzy as I walk there. I only feel somewhat queasy, but not enough to throw up.

Hallelujah!

When I climb back into bed, my phone goes off. It's Aiden. This is not his first time calling me. I've been ignoring him. At first, I ignored him because I didn't want to tell him that I might be pregnant. Now, I don't want to tell him that I am pregnant. The thing is that I need time. I need to get my head around this thing. I mean, how can I be pregnant? I mean, I know the mechanics of how this happened, but what does it mean now that I am? I need to have time to decide how I feel about this on my own. I don't want Aiden and his opinion getting in the way.

What if Aiden is really excited about this? I mean, would that make me excited as well? Probably. But is that right? I mean, all in all, I'm not ready to be a mom. I'm far from ready. I still have my own dreams and hopes and desires. But does that mean that only people without dreams and hopes should be parents? Of course not. And yet, I've always assumed that the only way that I would become a parent is when I gave up on my other life. None of these thoughts make any sense. I know that. And I need time to figure them out before I see Aiden again. I can't have him and his opinions muddling this whole thing for me, at least not any more than it already is.

And then, there is that other thought. What if...what if he doesn't want the baby? What if he is adamant and one-hundred percent certain that a baby is not for him? What then? What if he wants me to get rid of it? No, I can't have his opinions in my head right now. I need to decide how I feel about this baby first. And only then can I let him know what has happened.

The intercom goes off. I look down at my phone. More texts from Aiden appear, asking me where I am. Could that be him outside? No, please, no. I decide to ignore it. They'll just have to come over some other time. I'm not taking any visitors right now. But the buzzing continues. Incessantly. After a few minutes, I manage to drag myself out of bed and toward the front door.

"What?"

"Hey, Ellie," she says. My heart drops. I recognize her voice immediately.

CHAPTER 26 - ELLIE

WHEN SHE SHOWS UP…

"Are you okay?" I ask as soon as she walks through the door. I look her up and down. She looks normal. Her hair is cut in a short buzz cut. Her nails are painted black. She's dressed in tight jeans and a pair of Doc Marten boots. She has about five piercings in each ear, going all the way to the top of her earlobes, and a big forearm tattoo which I can only make out a little bit as it peeks out from under her shirt.

"Can I crash here for a bit?" Brie asks. "Mom and Dad are driving me nuts."

I inhale deeply. Well, that's a surprise, I think sarcastically.

"Sure, of course," I say quickly. "You're my sister."

Brie drags her large duffle bag into my living room and plops it down on my couch. She then heads to the refrigerator and opens it. I follow close behind her and quickly move her duffle bag to the floor - God only knows where this thing has been.

"Fuck, this thing is like a desert. How are you surviving?"

I shrug. "I haven't shopped for a while."

"Yeah, I can see that."

She looks into my freezer and helps herself to a pint of ice cream. Without bothering to get a plate, she just grabs a spoon and digs in.

If I weren't so used to this, I'd be offended. But this is just Brie Willoughby being Brie Willoughby. And no matter how different we are and how I'd never admit it out loud, or much less, to her directly, I've missed her.

Brie is my stepfather's daughter. My parents got divorced when I was eight and my mom started tutoring kids to make extra income. The pay was the best in Greenwich, Connecticut, where a lot of hedge fund managers and other finance people lived, and that's where she met Mitch. Mitch paid her $200 per hour to tutor Brie, who was five years old at the time. It's not that Brie was really behind on anything. It's just that everyone else's kids got tutored so it was expected by her school, to keep her from falling behind. Mom also said that Mitch wanted a warm female presence around his daughter after her mom died suddenly from cancer. Apparently, the slew of nannies that took care of her around the clock didn't exactly cut it. Mitch worked long hours and Brie was pretty much left alone except for the household help. Well, Mom started out as his household help but that didn't last long. They fell in love and, six months later, he asked her to marry him. They got married in Nantucket when I was eleven and Brie was nine.

"Mom and Dad are pretty awful sometimes, aren't they?" Brie asks, opening a box of cereal and shoving a big handful of it into her mouth.

"Do you want a bowl? Or milk?" I ask sarcastically.

"You don't have any milk."

"I have a bowl."

"No thanks."

I smile. Brie isn't the type to take people seriously who aren't being direct. And if you obfuscate your true intentions or passive aggressiveness, she will just go ahead and ignore that on purpose. I find it mildly annoying when she does it to me, but I find it hilarious when she does it to my mom who has her share of passive aggressive tendencies.

"So what are they doing this time?" I ask.

"Mom isn't happy about my new buzz cut, as you can imagine, but she won't come out and say it. Instead, she sent me pictures of a wig that I might like. A wig!"

I laugh. "Seriously?"

"It's like she thinks that I didn't get this hair cut because I wanted it. Like it's something that happened to be me."

"Well, you know Mom. Looking attractive is quite important to her," I say. Brie glares at me. "Not that I think you look unattractive. What I mean is that she is pretty conservative about what women should look like."

Wow, I really put my foot in my mouth with that one. But Brie just lets the whole thing run off her shoulders as if it's nothing. One of the reasons why she buzzed her hair is to not look like a regular girl. We both know that.

"So, what do you think about it?" she asks.

I look at her hair, or lack thereof. She's not completely bald, but it's definitely a close shave. I can see every nook and cranny in her skull.

"I like it."

"You liar."

"No, I like it because you like it. It's like you aren't wearing any armor. You don't have anything to hide behind. I've been noticing that you haven't been wearing much makeup recently either. Is it for the same reason?"

"Noticing? When? You haven't seen me in —"

"Months, I think," I say. "But I do follow you on Instagram and Snap."

"Oh, right." She shrugs.

"Yeah, well, I haven't really given it much thought.

But I guess there might be something to that. I've always felt like makeup created this barrier between you and the world. And it was always odd that only girls wore it. Like, why do we have to insulate ourselves against the world? When guys don't have to."

"Um...because we're women. And men are still in charge. Not as much as they once were, but for the most part," I say.

"Well, fuck that," Brie says.

"I agree."

"Hey, you know what Mom would say now?" Brie asks. I shake my head. "That men might be in charge, but it wouldn't hurt anything for me to go out there into the world looking attractive."

I laugh. "Yep, that's pretty much true."

"Of course, she never once stops to think about what attractive means. And how different cultures have different definitions of female beauty and beauty in general than we do."

I know exactly what she means. "Mom is pretty set

in her ways," I say. "So, what did Mitch say about this?"

Brie has called my mom *Mom* ever since she married Mitch, her dad. But because I still see my biological Dad and I still call him Dad, I never felt comfortable calling Mitch Dad, since he's not really.

Brie shrugs. "Nothing really. Dad couldn't care less."

"That's not true."

"Yes, it is. And you know, he just said he had to go to work. As always."

Mitch works a lot and not because we need the money. It's his way of surviving in the world. It's his way of checking out of difficult situations. Some people have drinking or drugs, others have yelling... Mitch has his work. He's a workaholic who probably needs to get treatment, but because it's so socially acceptable in this country to be addicted to working, no one thinks it's a big deal.

"I'm not sure Mom is just upset about my hair, though," Brie says after a moment, closing the box of Cheerios.

"What do you mean?"

"Eh, she wasn't exactly thrilled when I told her about the other thing I was thinking about."

"What?" I ask. She hesitates. "What? Tell me."

"You'll just get upset."

"No, I won't. I promise."

"You know how much I hate empty promises like that. I mean, you can't really promise not to get upset because you have no idea what I'm about to say."

I laugh. "You've been in college way too long," I say after a moment.

"Well, it's funny that you should bring that up. I'm actually thinking of taking a break."

"What?"

"Just for a semester. I want to go traveling. Central America, I think."

I shake my head. "But what about Swarthmore?"

She shrugs. "It'll still be there when I get back."

"But what about your friends? They'll all graduate before you."

"Well, many of them won't. People are already starting to take gap years just like they do in Europe. I think it's a really good idea. I mean, how the hell do we graduate and go out in the world without actually seeing any of it? How real people live."

I shrug. "You know me, I think travel is really important. I love to travel. But what about your education? Your degree?"

"My degree in anthropology will just have to wait," Brie says. "It's not exactly the most useful thing in the world."

I shake my head. "You know how much I hate statements like that. I mean, a university degree isn't just about its usability. What you learn in those classes defines you as a person, more than you'll ever know. I had no idea how much my contemporary literature class would influence my writing. Even though I just write romance."

"Oh, yeah!" Brie's eyes light up. "By the way, Mom told me about that. Holy fuck, Ellie! I got your books and...well, you've got quite an imagination."

I blush. I didn't exactly want to get into all that. No yet anyway.

CHAPTER 27 - ELLIE

WHEN I CAN'T HIDE THE TRUTH…

Brie is fascinated by my writing career or rather career. Not really sure what to call what I do at this point. It's not bringing in enough money to pay even half the rent on this place, but luckily I have the money that I got from Aiden. My heart skips a beat at just the thought of him. Everything is so different and he still doesn't know a thing. Mainly because I can't bring myself to tell him.

"So…how is all that going?" Brie asks.

"The writing? Really good actually, lots of people are buying the books, but, you know, it's not much money. The first one is only ninety-nine cents and

Amazon only pays me 30% from that. So I make about thirty cents from each book sold."

"Wow...that sucks."

"I have two other books in the series and they cost $2.99. I make 75% from that, but still, given how long it takes to write a book and how people mainly want to get free books or ninety-nine cent books, it's pretty hard to make a living."

"Do you do that Kindle Unlimited thing?"

"Yep."

"I joined. I like getting books from there."

"As an author, you have to be exclusive with them, so your books can't be anywhere else. And the pay? Well, it leaves much to be desired."

"How much?"

"$0.0045, the last time I checked. Less than half a cent per page read."

"How much is that?"

"About 90 cents for a 200 page book."

"Really?" Brie asks. "How the hell does anyone make any money?"

"They don't. Not really," I say with a shrug. "Unless you have a huge following. But in romance, it's really hard. All the readers want free books. Most readers also complain if a book is priced above 99 cents."

"Why the hell is that?" Brie asks. "I mean, everyone pays like four bucks for a cup of coffee at Starbucks and that's just some beans."

"Exactly. But for some reason, people think these books just fall out of the sky. Like it doesn't take me a month or so of hard work to write them. And I work alone. I mean, I have a proofreader, but I also do all the other self-publishing stuff alone. I make the covers and do the formatting and upload to Amazon. It all takes a lot of time and resources."

"So, why do you do it?"

"Because I love it. I love writing. I love this story. And I love the feedback that I get from the readers who are really into this series."

Brie nods. "I really hope I get some sort of passion like this."

"I sort of hope you don't," I say. "I've wanted to be a writer since I was a kid. I was obsessive about it. It's the only thing I ever imagined doing. And now? Well, I am doing it. People are buying the books, but I'm still not making much. Not like if I had a real job. But if I had a real job then I wouldn't be able to do this. And that's the paradox."

"Still, I wish I had a good answer for what I want to do with my life," Brie says. "Especially when Dad asks me the question."

I smile. Mitch is not one to keep his mouth shut about how worthless he thinks the anthropology degree from Swarthmore is.

"So, let me get this straight," I say. "He doesn't approve of your major but he still doesn't want you to take a semester off to travel?"

"He says that he'd be fine with it if I was going to study abroad, took classes, but not just to travel. I don't know what his problem is, Ellie."

I do. He's a dad. He doesn't want his little girl tramping around some third world country all alone. It would make him feel a lot better if she went there through some program with some other equally idealistic kids her age. But I can't say any of this to her right now. I have a new wave of nausea come over me and I barely make it to the bathroom.

The sheer volume of vomit is no longer the same as it was. So, the anti-nausea medication is definitely working, but it hasn't taken it away completely.

"Are you okay?" Brie knocks on the door and then comes in when I don't reply. I wonder if I should lie for now or tell her the truth.

But she picks up the bottle of Diclegis from the bathroom sink. "Why do you have this?" she asks.

"Why?" I ask, not sure how I should respond.

"Ellie, this is anti-nausea medication that Kim Kardashian took when she was pregnant."

"Oh, really?" I play dumb. "And how do you know that? I didn't know you cared so much about reality stars."

"I don't. But no matter how much I try to block out contemporary culture it still seeps in," Brie says. "Now, don't avoid the question. Why the hell are you taking this?"

"Because the over-the-counter stuff didn't work," I say after a moment and bury my head in the toilet.

Brie stares at me. I wipe my mouth and get up off the floor. I grab my toothbrush and brush my teeth. I glance at Brie in the mirror and note the deer-in-the-headlights look on her face. Perhaps there were more sensitive ways of telling her the big news. The problem is that she will be the first one to know and I'm not entirely sure that's right. If anyone should be the first to know about this, it is the father of the baby. The problem is that I still haven't made up my mind how I feel about all of this.

"You're...pregnant?" she asks after a moment. I wipe my mouth on the towel hanging behind me and nod.

"Ellie?" she asks, seeking further confirmation.

"Yes," I finally say, turning to face her. "I'm pregnant."

CHAPTER 28 - ELLIE

WHEN WE TALK ABOUT IT...

Brie is more stunned about the pregnancy news than I honestly thought she would be. I am only three years older, but we have always been on somewhat different wavelengths on just about everything in our lives. In many ways, she is more courageous than I am. She's the one who wants to stand up to our parents and challenge their world views by going out on her own. On the other hand, she readily admits that she's lost. She wants to travel because school doesn't feel right anymore and she's scared of graduating. Graduation is an end point and, without a firm plan, there isn't really much to do afterward. It's decision time and she's not ready.

"You know you don't have to have your life figured out at twenty-two," I say to her over a cup of hot tea. "I know that all those people in your class who have plans for graduate school or law school or have jobs lined up. They make it seem so easy. They make it look like it's no big deal. But it is. It is a big decision and a big deal."

"Thanks for taking the pressure off, sis," Brie says sarcastically.

"You know what I mean."

"No, not really."

"Okay, what I mean is that many people your age feel like, if they don't have it all together, if they don't know what to do with their life right at this moment, like it's all over or something. Like you're going to waste your time or make a mistake. And all I want to say is that it's okay to make mistakes. It's okay to not know where you are headed. Because you'll figure it out eventually."

"Like you?"

"Haha. I guess you figured me out. I'm saying this as much for me as for you."

"You don't have it figured out?" Brie asks.

"Not even close."

"What are you thinking?"

She wants to know what I'm going to do about the pregnancy. I don't have the faintest idea.

"I don't know," I say after a moment. "But making myself crazy about what this all means for my life isn't going to help any. That's what I've been doing this whole time since I found out and it hasn't gotten me anywhere."

"And where do you want to go?" Brie asks.

I think about that for a moment. "I've never thought of that before. Hmm, I don't know. The thing is that I never really wanted to be a mom."

"You didn't?" Brie asks.

I shake my head. Brie and I are sisters but we're not like many other girls out there. We didn't spend our childhoods talking about weddings, babies, and marriage. No, we made up stories and played pretend. But rarely about relationships.

"Did you?" I ask.

"Actually, I did," she says after a moment. "I do, I mean."

"Really? You want to be a mom?"

"Well, maybe not right now, but I think it will be kind of cool, you know? To have a little kid to play with."

"You don't just play with them you know," I say. "They're a ton of work."

Brie gives me a mysterious coy smile.

"What?" I ask. "What's that about?"

"I know you, Ellie. And I know that right now all you're thinking about is all the things that you won't be able to do with a baby. Like you think you won't be able to be yourself anymore. That the baby will make you some sort of mom-character. And as this mom-character, you'll have to sublimate everything about yourself. Like you'll have to get a minivan, a house in the suburbs, and a mortgage. Maybe you'll even have to cut your hair."

Shit. Holy mother-fucking shit. She's spot on in her analysis. I have actually thought all of these things.

"But those are just the decorative things about what it means to be a mom. Just because other people are like that, it doesn't mean that you have to be. It doesn't mean that that's the kind of life you have to lead."

I nod and look away. My eyes are actually watering and I don't want her to see me cry.

"You don't have to cut your hair just because you have a baby, Ellie," Brie says, putting her arm around me. A big tear rolls down my cheek. She wipes it away and gives me a kiss on the forehead.

"It's so stupid," I finally say. "But I actually thought those things."

"I know you did."

"I don't know why," I mumble. "I mean, I know… rationally, that I'm in charge of my life. And plenty of people have good lives - fulfilling lives - with kids. And that the kids just add to their lives. But whenever I see kids out there with their parents… well, they just seem so all-encompassing, all-consuming that I feel like the parents are drowning."

"But your kid doesn't have to be that way. I mean,

you get to make your relationship with him or her as you see fit. At least, until they're in high school." Brie laughs.

"So, you think I will still have time to write with a baby?" I ask.

"Of course you will. They sleep a hell of a lot and that will be your time to yourself."

"And what about traveling? I've always loved to go to new places."

"Well, now you'll have a little person to go with you. How fun would that be?"

I shrug. I never thought of it that way. Like this little baby can be my companion.

"Remember Charlie?" Brie asks. How could I forget? Charlie was my old dog. "You two used to go everywhere together. You even took her camping when you drove out to Montana with your boyfriend. And she wasn't an easy dog to take places."

Tears roll down my cheeks. I miss Charlie so much; my heart breaks into a million pieces just thinking about her. But Brie is right. I did take Charlie everywhere and she wasn't exactly a friendly dog. She was a spaniel who didn't like anyone. Not other people. Not other dogs. That pretty much meant that when we traveled together, I couldn't really take her inside any establishments.

"I'm a firm believer that if you made traveling work with Charlie, the baby will be a breeze. Man, she was a handful."

I smile through the tears.

"The thing is, Ellie, I'm not trying to convince you to go either way with this decision. It's your body and your life. But I just don't want you thinking that this baby will consume your life for the worse. You will still be able to be you. You will still be able to pursue your dreams and do what you want. Being a mom won't change who you are at your core, no matter what television shows and movies try to tell you. It will be challenging and tiring at times, but it will also be wonderful. It may the best thing that will ever happen to you."

"I really appreciate it," I say, giving her a warm hug. "And thanks for making this decision easier," I add sarcastically. Brie laughs.

WE SPEND the afternoon sitting around and gabbing. I haven't laughed this hard in a really long time. Not since...Caroline. We order some Indian food and put on *Thelma and Louise* as we wait for dinner to come.

"This movie is amazing," Brie says. "Way ahead of its time. We talked about it both in my film class and my women's studies class."

"It's one of my favorites. And Brad Pitt isn't too hard on the eyes in it either."

"I think this is one of his earliest roles."

When the buzzer goes off, Brie gets the food and pays the delivery man. The bags immediately fill the house with the aroma of curry, making my mouth salivate. Unfortunately, a moment later, I find myself running to the bathroom to puke. I refuse to come out until Brie sticks the food out onto the balcony or the refrigerator. When I do finally emerge, I can still smell it.

"Wow, you're really sick," Brie says.

"Yeah, and this is with taking four pills a day."

"Is there anything else you can do?"

I shake my head, no. "Without the pills, I'd probably be in the emergency room getting fluids. Kate Middleton was like this. I think she ended up at the hospital. Listen, I don't want to talk about this."

"Okay," Brie says. "So what do you want to talk about?"

I shrug.

"So, what are you going to do?" she asks after a moment. I shrug again.

"Listen, that was a great talk and all and I totally see your point. But I still have no idea what I'm going to do about this pregnancy. I still have no idea if it's the right thing for me, at this moment."

Brie nods.

"Besides, whatever I do, I have to tell the father first."

"Oh, Aiden Black," Brie says.

I furrow my brow. I don't like the tone with which she says his name.

"Yes?" I say. "You don't approve?"

She shakes her head.

"Oh, c'mon, Brie. You haven't even met him."

"Okay, fine. I'll give you that. But, Ellie, the CEO of Owl? Really?"

"At least, he's got a job," I say.

"Whatever." She shakes her head. She hasn't approved of many of my boyfriends, but something is different about her attitude toward Aiden.

"What's wrong?" I ask. She shrugs. "Brie?"

"Okay, fine. You know that he's a playboy, right? You know about his reputation? I mean, he must've dated every woman in the Victoria's Secret catalog, going back a decade."

"He's a nice guy, Brie."

"His reputation is worse than Leonardo DiCaprio's when it comes to womanizing."

"Brie, he's a really good guy, okay? He hasn't cheated on me. Yes, he dated a lot of models in the past. And I definitely don't look like one. But... I don't know, we have this connection."

"What kind of connection?"

I try to explain how Aiden and I feel about each other, but it doesn't really come out right. It's hard to put into words.

"Besides, he's not a creep or anything, if you're thinking that. He doesn't molest or hit on women who aren't interested. If you're worried about him being accused of that by the #MeToo movement, you don't have to worry."

"I just thought that he was a horn-dog," Brie says after a moment. "I didn't think he assaulted anyone."

"Okay, good. Well, I just wanted to make that clear."

That's when Blake and Tom pop into my head. Brie doesn't know anything about that part of my life. And it's about to become a lot more public, so I decide to come clean. I start with the auction, at the beginning, and talk for close to an hour without an interruption. Brie listens carefully before reaching over and giving me a warm embrace.

"I'm really sorry," she whispers, her eyes wet with tears. "I can't believe you went through all of that... and you didn't tell me about it earlier."

"We just haven't been talking much lately," I say. "And frankly, I was a little embarrassed."

"So, Caroline killed herself after all, huh?"

I nod. This is the first person outside of Aiden who knows the truth. But she won't be the last.

"You know, I might not know this Aiden Black, but I think he did the right thing telling the DA about Caroline. I think that leaving that letter was her way of letting you know that she really did want people to know. She just needed help sharing it with the world."

I nod. I know she's right, I just hate it.

CHAPTER 29 - ELLIE

After spending my morning with my head buried in the toilet, I bring my laptop into bed with me and open my last project. It's the next book in the auction series. I skim over the last 3,000 words that I've written to refresh my memory and look over the notes that I made before I got sick. Well, not sick exactly. It's not like being pregnant is being sick, but it's definitely not being well. Everything seems in order. I have the next chapter all laid out. I type up the notes on what I want to cover and start the timer. I always write in twenty minute intervals. That way if nothing comes out, I only write for twenty minutes and the whole process doesn't seem that overwhelming. But usually I just keep going. Twenty minutes quickly turns into forty and then sixty. Typically, I manage to get through three sessions before I get tired or need to take a break. Not this time though.

I sit in front of my computer and stare at the cursor. Nothing comes to mind. I mean, everything is planned out, but words are just so hard to come by. I sit staring at the blank page for exactly six minutes and thirty nine seconds before I give up and stop the timer.

"Shit," I say. This is much worse than I thought. I mean, I knew that the nausea made it hard to walk around and function as a person, but I didn't know that it would actually have an effect on my brain. It's not that I feel particularly tired this morning. I just feel...drained.

Then I do what any writer should never do. Turn on Facebook and read my

Newsfeed. When I get bored, I follow that up with about ten articles on BuzzPost. I even take a few of their useless quizzes, the ones I used to write. I find out that I should retire in Belize based on the type of kitchen I like and that I should paint my house white based on the number of pets I have (or don't have as it is in my case). I avoid the quiz about how many kids I will have based on the kind of 90's shows I like. That one just hits a little bit too close to home.

And then something occurs to me. I'm not sure where it comes from except that the idea formulates somewhere in the back of my head. It's a story about a guy who loves his family and child, but feels trapped by the whole thing. Trapped because he has to work as a teacher when he really wants to be a writer. One day, he goes on a run and stumbles upon the body of a dead girl. When he's about to call the police, he sees a large suitcase full of cash next to her. The bag contains over two million dollars. He takes it and that's when things start to go bad for him. It's just a kernel of an idea. I don't really have any idea of where it will go or why, but I quickly pick up a piece of paper and start outlining. I write down what happens in chapter after chapter and the ideas just pour out of me. It reminds me of the time when I was writing my first romance book, about the auction. It was true to what really happened and then I thought that the words came so easily because I didn't have to make anything up. Yet now, I'm making up every last bit and the story is unfolding just as fast. I must be onto something.

An hour later, the outline for *The Dead Girl* is complete. I have no idea why I'm working on this. I doubt that it's going to go anywhere. I mean, I don't even have a thriller name, a brand, or even a mailing list, and yet it feels exciting just to think about working on it. There's something intriguing about a man who finds a bag of money and sees it as an escape from his life. And yet, after going through all of that drama and action, what he realizes at the end is that what he really wants is to have his family again.

"Ellie, there's someone here to see you!" Brie yells from the living room. I have gotten so involved in my story, with instrumental pop music blaring in my earphones, that I didn't hear the door.

"Hey," he says. I turn around and see Aiden standing in my doorway. I glance over at Brie who is hovering behind him, with her arms crossed at her chest. She is clearly not approving of this.

"Oh, hey," I mumble.

"Ellie, what's going on?" Aiden asks. "I've been calling. And texting."

"I know."

"Didn't you want to see me?"

"Didn't you get my texts?" I ask.

He shrugs. "Yes, of course. But all you said was that you couldn't see me that day."

I have been unfair. I've been pushing Aiden away and not explaining a thing. But that's because I needed to buy time. I needed time to figure some things out.

I look up at him. Wow, I had somewhat forgotten how handsome he really is. That thick, gorgeous hair. Those large eyes and long eyelashes. They're almost feminine in their delicateness, conveying both depth and sorrow. He just came from work - lunch hour? - so he's still dressed in one of his perfectly tailored gray suits, which hugs his toned body in just the right way.

"Aiden, that's my sister, Brie."

"Yes, we've met," he says.

"Ellie, do you want me to get him out of here?" Brie asks. I smile. I like her no-nonsense way of being. People never took her seriously, but that haircut really gives her an edge. By the look on Aiden's face, I can tell that he's taking her seriously.

"No, it's fine," I say.

"Are you sure?"

I nod.

"Well, just let me know," she says. "I'll be in the kitchen."

"Your sister is scary," Aiden says, half-jokingly.

"Yes, she is." I nod.

He walks over and sits down on the bed next to me. "Ellie, what's going on?" he asks. "I'm really sorry about whatever it is that I did. I thought that everything was okay between us."

"Yes, it's fine," I mumble. I take a deep breath. There's no getting out of it. I have to tell him.

"So? Why have you been avoiding me?"

"Aiden, I have to tell you something."

"You're pregnant?" Aiden asks. I have already explained this to him twice and yet he still seems to have trouble processing it.

"Listen, like I said, you don't have to be involved."

"What do you mean not be involved?" he asks.

I shrug. I don't know how he feels about this and I'm not sure if I want to.

"Of course I'm going to be here for you, Ellie," Aiden says. "I love you."

And with that simple phrase, the weight of the world suddenly lifts off my shoulders. I've run through a million different reactions in my head, but this one, frankly never came to mind.

"Ellie?" Aiden asks. I stare at him in disbelief.

"I don't understand."

"Ellie, I'm so...happy. I never really thought about having kids, honestly. But, now that you're pregnant. I'm genuinely happy."

"Really?"

"Are you not?"

I don't know. I've been so worried about what I should be thinking and feeling that I haven't given much thought to what I was actually thinking and feeling. And reality? Well, after having that long talk with Brie, I felt okay about it. Maybe even a little excited. Perhaps, it will be fine after all.

"I don't know," I say.

"Well, I know that it's your decision, but if you want to hear my thoughts…" Aiden says.

I stare at him, waiting for him to continue.

"I'm really happy about it. I'd love to have a baby with you. I love you. And I want to be a family."

Family. Oh my God. That word sends a shiver through my body. But when I look up at him, suddenly it all feels aright.

"I'm sorry I've been ignoring your calls," I say. "I was just so worried about this. Worried and sick."

"I wish you had told me. I mean, it must be hard trying to decide how you feel about this, throwing up so much like you are."

I nod. He has a point. I've never been much of the mothering type, but being this sick all the time definitely hasn't helped matters. For one thing, I felt depressed and down most of the day. I had never felt this way before. I thought that my feelings of melancholy came from the actual physical experience of being pregnant, but in reality they didn't. I think they came from all the hormonal changes and the fact that I was throwing up all the time.

"I'm just so...confused," I finally admit the truth. "I mean, one minute I think it's going to be okay and the next, I'm completely freaking out."

Aiden nods and takes me into his arms. He kisses the top of my head and tells me that it's going to be okay. And then he just holds me. He doesn't ask me any more questions or force me to put what I'm feeling into words. He just holds me and makes me feel like it's all going to be okay. I breathe in and out and after a few minutes, I believe him.

"Listen, Ellie, whatever you decide, I'm here for you. I want you to know that," he says after a while. "I love you."

"I love you, too," I mumble into his shirt.

"But I also want you to know that the thought of this baby...well, it makes me excited. I always thought that I would freak out or run away. That there was no way that I would ever have a kid, but now that it's here...well, it feels ok. Right even. It feels like it's something that should happen."

I breathe in and out deeply.

"I don't want to put any pressure on you. I'm not saying this to sway you either way. Please know that. I'm just telling you because I want you to know how I feel. To really know how I truly feel."

I nod. Were it anyone else in his position, I'd say it was bullshit - that the guy was just saying that to guilt me into having the baby. But by the earnest expression on Aiden's face, I know that he's telling me the truth. There are no ulterior motives here. No obfuscation. No lies. It's the whole truth, and nothing but the truth.

"So...what does this mean?" I ask slowly.

"It means that the decision is all yours. And I will support you no matter what."

I inhale deeply. It's crazy to think that only a minute ago I was so confused by what I should do. And now? Well, just the fact that he was into it, and not just into it, actually excited by the whole thing, well, that made me feel okay about it. Like, perhaps, this is something that I could really do - become a mom. Now, there's a trip!

"I have to tell you something," Aiden says, pulling away. The expression on his face grows serious and my heart sinks. Now what's wrong?

"I have my job at Owl back for good."

"You what?" I ask. I can hardly believe it.

"Yep, they want me back. Apparently, no one else can run it as well as I do."

"Oh my God." I throw my arms around his neck and give him a big kiss. He kisses me right back, so passionately that my knees grow weak. We fall into bed together with him on top of me.

"I guess we'll have to postpone our trip to Belize for a bit," Aiden says, pulling slightly away. He brushes my hair out of my face and gives me a little peck on the cheek.

"I guess so," I say sadly. "If only I wasn't so sick."

"Well, you have a date there. As soon as you feel better, I'll take time off and I'll take you there. On a proper vacation."

"I'd like that," I whisper.

Aiden presses his lips to mine and I let his tongue make its way inside. I had forgotten what a good and gentle kisser he is. These are the kind of kisses that will make you forget just about everything in life, except maybe the one thing that I can't forget - that I'm about to be a mom.

CHAPTER 30 - AIDEN

I've never given having a baby much thought. I mean, there were those scares early on when I was just starting my business. A girl I had a one-night stand with thought she might be pregnant. And my ex-wife. But they turned out to be nothing. Just a period that was a few days late. Those were the longest days of my life though. And as much as I knew that I would have to step up and be a father, I also realized that there was no way in hell I could be one. I would pay alimony - a lot of alimony - but that was all I could offer them. Maybe an occasional visit. Man was I happy that those scares never really materialized into anything.

And today? Well, today, hearing about Ellie? A part

of me was terrified that I would feel the same way. I never grew up around many kids, let alone babies. So, the thought of having one myself, one that belongs to me, scared the hell out of me. But when Ellie came out and said that she was pregnant and that I wouldn't have to participate if I didn't want to, well, it just felt wrong. I don't know if this is just me being older or the fact that I'm with Ellie, but the stars seemed to have aligned. Suddenly, I'm just not scared. I'm actually excited. I'm looking forward to it. That is if she decides to have it.

It's Ellie's decision after all. And I'm okay with it. There's no way I want to bring a child into this world whose mother isn't happy to have him or her. There are way too many unwanted children as it is and there's nothing really worse than for a child to grow up unloved - even though it happens all too often.

Ellie runs past me to throw up in the bathroom, again. I want to hold up her hair and help her in any way I can, but she won't let me. She doesn't want me to see her "like that." Silly girl. Little does she know that I'm in love with her, every last gross bit of her. And no amount of disgusting excrement that comes out of her will change any of it.

"Can you not be here?" she says as I stand next to the bathroom door asking how she's feeling for the millionth time.

"Okay, I'm sorry. I just want to make sure you're okay."

I walk away and sit down on her bed. I check my emails on my phone when I hear her call my name.

"Yeah?" I get up to walk over.

"Don't come over."

"Okay...So, why are you calling me?"

"Because, I just wanted to say that I've decided what I'm going to do!" she yells and throws up again.

My heart sinks. This can't be good. No wise decisions were ever made with someone's head in the toilet.

"I'm going to keep it," Ellie says. "We're going to have a baby!"

I can't believe my ears. I run into the bathroom and wrap my arms around her. She tries to push me away, but I don't let her.

"I love you," I whisper, holding her hair back.

"I love you," she manages to say.

I CALL off work for the afternoon and spend it in bed with her. It's not exactly as romantic of a time as we've previously had, but it's special in its own way. I stroke her hair as we watch an episode of *The Office* and laugh.

"Thank you for taking care of me," Ellie says as one episode ends and the next one starts. "And thank you for...being you."

"Thank you for being you," I whisper.

"Oh, man, can we get any more sappy?" she jokes.

"Yes," I say after a moment. "I could ask you to marry me again."

She looks up at me, not sure if I'm joking. I am, but only partly.

"Will you marry me, Ellie?" I ask.

"Are you serious?" she asks. I nod.

"Oh, c'mon, Aiden." Ellie gets up. "Why did you have to ask me when I have vomit on my shirt?"

"Because I don't care. And from the looks of it, this phase in your pregnancy might last well into the next one, which will also involve a lot of vomit on your shirt."

"What do you mean?"

"The baby? They're known to spit up once in a while, too."

Ellie shakes her head.

"Okay, if you don't like this, that's fine. I'll ask you again. Later. In a more romantic setting."

Ellie looks away from me. For a few minutes no one says a word. Suddenly, it occurs to me that I have made a terrible mistake. Women don't like things like this. They like drama and pomp. They like to celebrate important moments in their lives in heels and tight dresses instead of sweatshirts and dirty hair. Fuck.

"I really messed up, didn't I?" I ask.

She doesn't respond. I put my hand on her shoulder

and turn her to face me. That's when I see the tears running down her face.

"What's wrong? Ellie? I'm so sorry," I whisper.

"No, nothing's wrong. Nothing at all," she mumbles through the tears.

I stare at her, not quite sure of what to say next.

"You are just so...wonderful. I really don't deserve you, Aiden Black."

"What are you talking about?"

"Here I am wearing my pajamas. I just threw up about a billion times and I'm not wearing a smidge of makeup. And what do you do? You ask me to marry you."

"That's because you're the most beautiful woman in the world and I'm in love with you."

My words bring tears to her eyes.

"So, what do you say?" I ask after a moment.

"I don't want to just get married because I'm pregnant," she says.

"That's not why I'm asking you. I've asked you before, if you remember."

Of course, she remembers. Ellie stares out in the distance. Does she really want to marry me? Is this the right thing to do?

"Yes," she finally says. "I will marry you."

"Oh, Ellie," I say, wrapping her arms around me. "I love you."

I press my lips onto hers and the world outside stops spinning. Nothing else matters except for this moment.

I wrap my hands around her breasts and enjoy the plumpness. Then I run my tongue down her neck and along her collarbone. She tilts her head back with pleasure, exposing more of her neck. I pull her shirt over her head and take off her bra. I press her nipples in between my teeth and bite down slightly. She moans with pleasure.

I push her down on the bed and pull off her pants and panties. Then I take off my shirt and drop my pants, along with my boxer shorts. She licks her lips as I climb on top of her. I lick her nipples again and quickly make my way down her body. I pause briefly at her belly button and admire her body as she arches her back. But I keep heading south. I run my tongue along her non-existent panty line. Her hipbones come up to meet my lips and kiss them as well. Her legs open up on their own and I make my way down in between her thighs. Once she's lying bare before me, I can't contain myself anymore. I have to have her. I spread her thighs and thrust my tongue deep within her. She moans with pleasure and I press my fingers on her clit. Then I start to massage her and she starts to moan louder. When she is getting close, I push myself up and push my penis inside of her.

"Oh, Aiden!" Ellie yells into my ear. I thrust in and out of her faster and faster. She yells my name even louder and a wave of ecstasy courses through my body. It comes sooner than I had planned, but I ride the wave anyway. There's no turning back now.

"Oh, Ellie," I moan and collapse on top of her.

CHAPTER 31 - AIDEN

WHEN HE SURPRISES ME…

Lying next to her in the afterglow of our lovemaking, I wrap one of her long strands of hair around my finger. We are actually engaged. I'm not sure if we will get married before or after the baby, but I'm overjoyed by the prospect that we actually will. I'm going to have a wife. No, that doesn't sound as good as it could. Ellie is going to be my wife. Now, that's much better.

"You have beautiful hair," I whisper. Her eyes are closed, but she's not asleep. She gives me a little smile without stirring.

"Ellie?"

"Hmmm?"

"I don't really want to bring this up again, but I sort of have to," I say, choosing my words carefully. Not only do I not want to bring it up, but this is the last thing I want to talk about.

"Okay," she mumbles and turns away from me. "I'm listening."

I take a deep breath. This did not go well the last time we talked about it.

"What do you think about the whole Caroline thing?" I ask. She turns around to face me.

I don't say anything else. Instead, I wait for her to answer.

"I think you did the right thing," she says. "I'm sorry I got so upset last time."

I nod. "I wasn't fishing for an apology."

"I know," she says. "But I was thinking about it and I think you're right. Caroline could've easily not told me a thing about her on-purpose overdose. She could've gone to her grave that way. But she didn't.

She wanted someone to know the truth. I'm just sorry that person had to be me."

"You would've rather thought that she died by accident?"

"I don't know," she says, shrugging. "I just really miss my friend. But I want Tom to pay for what he did. I want him to suffer."

"So if the DA wants you to come in for a statement?" I ask.

"I'll go to Maine."

I smile. I'm glad that she feels this way. I don't want Tom to get away with what he did any more than I want Blake to get away with it.

"That sort of brings me to the other district attorney conversation," I say. "My attorney said that the DA is planning on pressing charges against Blake for what happened on the yacht. Or at least, he's trying to build a case."

She nods, without meeting my gaze. Being involved in this case is much more difficult. She is the victim here. And though Tom attacked her at the

Warrenhouse's party as well, it wasn't a sexual attack. Sexual attacks are always more difficult to talk about, especially for women. They are more sensitive. They are more embarrassing.

"I know that this is so stupid," Ellie says after a long pause. "But I just feel like such an idiot about what happened. I mean, I know that it's not my fault, but it feels like it is."

"It's not! Not at all. He attacked you. You were completely helpless."

"Yeah, I know that. Intellectually. But not down here," Ellie says, pointing to her heart. "And not down here," she adds, pointing to her gut.

"Ellie—" I try to find words that will make the pain go away.

"That's probably how Caroline felt," she says. "Terrified, petrified, and mortified. And what Blake did to me, well that was nothing in comparison to what Tom did."

I nod. I wish there was something I could do to take all the pain away. But while I try to figure out what that is, I wrap my arms around her and press her close to me.

"Do you want me to kill him?" I ask, only half-joking. She waits for a moment before answering. "No, if anyone should do it, I should do it."

We both laugh a little bit. I don't know about her, but after everything he has put us through, I'm not even half-joking. It's more like five percent joking, ninety-five percent not joking.

"What do you think you want to do about Blake?" I ask.

"I'm going to talk to the DA. I want to press charges, if he thinks my testimony is enough for that. Blake is a bad guy and everyone needs to know what he did to me."

"And about the auction?" I ask. "All of that is going to come out."

"I won't do it, if you don't want me to," she says.

"Oh, hell no. Please don't misunderstand. I want him to pay. And, frankly, I don't really care if all that shit about the auction comes out. It was just a little game.

Everyone consented. Everyone was of age. No one got paid to have sex with anyone. Even if they did, that's not what they were paid for, legally. My attorneys can spin it any which way and the public relations people will do the rest. I'm just concerned about you. How you're going be going through all of this."

"I'll be fine," she says.

"Promise me one thing, okay, Ellie?" I ask. "Promise me that if you ever feel hopeless, lost, or depressed that you will come to me and tell me. I will get you help. I will help you. I will be here for you no matter what."

"I promise," she says a little too quickly.

"I just never want you to feel the way Caroline did. I mean, how horrible she must've felt to do what she did. It just breaks my heart."

"Me, too," she says with a tear running down her cheek.

"I'm here for you, Ellie. No matter what. Please come to me with anything, no matter what. You're not alone."

Ellie leans over to kiss me.

"I think I'm going to be sick," she says. The serene expression on her face vanishes as she gets up to run to the bathroom.

THE COLD AIR hit me like a truck as soon as I stepped outside. Is this winter ever going to end? I imagine lying on the deck of my yacht in the Caribbean with Ellie and my heart yearns for it. She can throw up just as well down there as she can here. But at least it would be warm and nice out. And I can walk around in flip-flops without a t-shirt instead of a pair of heavy winter boots, two sweaters, a coat, a hat, and a scarf. Fuck, I hate the cold.

Winter always looks like this magical, wonderful time of the year in magazines and in the movies. But in reality, it's a black, slushy mess. It requires way too many clothes and the darkness makes everyone depressed and unhappy. The days never last long enough at all. Sometimes, it's so cloudy that the sun doesn't even make an appearance for days.

I know that I shouldn't moan about this. I'm very

lucky. I have my job back. I have a baby on the way. And my girlfriend finally agreed to marry me. The beginning of the year has started out magnificently for me. And yet, I can't help but wonder how much better I'd feel if the sun was shining all the time and it was seventy-five degrees out.

I trot over to the bagel place at the end of the street. It's not far enough away to drive to and I can't possibly hail a cab or get an Uber for such a short distance. Yet, walking a whole city block in this cold is a significant exercise.

"Aiden!" someone yells behind me. "Aiden!"

I know his voice. How could I not? But I don't want to turn around. I just want him to leave. Why the fuck can't he just leave me alone?

"You were at Ellie's house," Blake says. It's more of a statement than a question. "Why won't you turn around? Are you too chicken-shit to face me?"

"No, I'm not," I say. Unlike last time, Blake isn't drunk. He's fully in control of himself and he's still an asshole.

"Don't tell me you and Ellie are...together."

"Yes, we are."

"The papers made it seem like you were just fucking."

"We are."

I don't know why I'm engaging with him about this. I don't really care. Except that he was once a very important person in my life. He was one of my closest friends. My confidant. The only person who knew what it was like to grow Owl from my dorm room to what it is now, the biggest competitor to Amazon.

"What are you doing, Blake?" I ask. "Why are you here?"

"I'm here to see Ellie."

"You can't."

"Yes, I can!"

"Blake, please. Go home."

"The DA is pressing charges," he says. "Do you know

that? Your bitch of a girlfriend is going to testify against me."

"Listen, why don't you just go and fuck yourself?" I say as calmly as possible. He's looking to get a rise out of me. And it's working. My blood is starting to boil. I take a deep breath. As much as I want to punch him in the throat, I can't get into a fight right now. I just got my job back at Owl. It's still a tenuous situation. I'm not sure how long I will hold onto it if the shareholders see a picture of me in some gossip magazine punching out the previous CEO. No, you have to stay calm, Aiden, I say to myself. You're going to get some fresh bagels and tea, so keep walking. I turn around and pick up my step.

"Hey! Hey! You think you're too good for me?"

I ignore him.

"I insult your girlfriend and you just keep walking. Who the fuck do you think you are?"

Keep going, Aiden, I say to myself.

"I'm three times the man that you are. I should've had my way with her when I had the chance so that now she'd know what she is missing."

That's it. I turn around and lunge at him. I toss him onto the ground and start to pound him in the face. The first few blows send shockwaves through my hands. I haven't punched anyone like this in...ages. Actually, I've never punched anyone like this. But I haven't been in a fight since middle school.

A few of my punches miss and my balled up fists collide with the pavement. My whole body aches from the shock.

"Fuck!" I scream in his face. I pull away from him and stare at the limp body of my ex-best friend laying before me. For a moment, I'm not sure if he's dead. My heart jumps into my chest. No, no, no. Please don't be dead. Please, please, please.

That's when I see his chest moving up and down with each labored breath.

Okay, good. He's okay.

I look around. There are not that many people out, but it's not like the street is completely deserted. If I go back to Ellie's now, this whole thing will just blow over. And if he's seriously hurt? Well, someone is bound to come by and help. There's no way that I'm going to be making that call to the police.

I force myself to my feet. My whole body aches.

"Fuck you, Blake," I say and stagger past him back in the direction of Ellie's apartment.

And then...everything turns to black.

CHAPTER 32 - ELLIE

Aiden went to get tea and bagels half an hour ago. Then an hour ago. Then two hours ago. Then two hours and forty-five minutes. Where the hell can he be? I crawl out of bed and force myself to go out to the living room. Brie is sitting in front of the television watching a Real Housewives of Beverly Hills marathon. I think that show is crap and yet I can't not watch it. It was one of Caroline's favorites and it's one of my all-time guilty pleasures.

Where could he be? As my nausea subsides, my worry about Aiden increases. I'm not one to worry unnecessarily. At least, I try to keep my worries at bay. But this time, I have a bad feeling about everything. It came over me about twenty minutes after Aiden left and hasn't disappeared since.

I call his phone for what feels like the tenth time since he left. This time I don't ask him to call me back.

"Listen, if you needed to go to work or something, that's fine. I'm totally okay with it. Just please call or text and let me know. For some reason, I got really worried. I don't know, maybe it's all the pregnancy hormones. Just let me know what's going on."

I pace around my room. When I hear Brie out in the kitchen, I meet her there.

"So...you and Aiden?" Brie gives me a wink over her buttered toast. "How's that working out?"

I shrug and smile.

"Pretty good from what I heard last night."

I blush. I didn't realize that we were loud enough to hear. Brie must sense my embarrassment.

"Hey, it's no big deal," she says, waving her hand.

Brie and I are close, but not close the way sisters are often portrayed in sappy movies. For some reason, we were never the type to lay around at night gushing about what this or that guy said to us. Or gal, for that matter. I sort of suspect that Brie may be a lesbian, but because we're not that close, I don't feel comfortable bringing it up.

"We were sort of celebrating something," I say after a moment.

"What?"

"Aiden asked me to marry him."

"Okay…" she says slowly. "I thought that he had already asked you that?"

Oh, that's right. She knows about the previous failed engagement. Not everything, but enough.

"Well, he asked again," I say.

"Does he know about the baby?"

"Of course, he does. I told him about it and…he was actually much more excited about it than I thought he would be."

"Oh, that's great, Ellie."

"I think so," I say and go into the long-winded

account of what happened. How I told him. What he said. What I said. How he asked me to marry him. She listens carefully and then throws her arms around me.

"I'm so happy for you."

"I'm genuinely surprised. I mean, I really didn't expect to be a basket-case about this whole thing. What do you think? I feel like such an idiot."

"An idiot? Why?"

"I don't know. Just feel sort of stupid. I mean, I should be more excited about having a baby."

"You're just young. And you're thinking of the way that it's going to affect your life in a negative way. But maybe you shouldn't. Maybe you should think about all the good that will come out of it. All the fun."

"That's the problem," I say. "I don't really have any experience with kids. I mean, I don't know any babies. Aiden doesn't have much family and we never had any babies around. It's just a weird thing to imagine having a baby when you have no personal experience with one."

"I know exactly what you mean."

Brie is also not exactly the mothering type. But then again, maybe that's not a requirement. Actually, I know for sure that it's not a requirement to be a mother. But are those skills something you should acquire in order to actually become a good mother? Probably. And will they come naturally? Or is there some sort of class I should take?

I graduated from Yale and there wasn't one course in the catalog about anything like this. Perhaps, that's the tragedy since most of the kids I went to school with grew up in terrible homes. Not terrible as in abusive, but terrible in that they felt neglected and ignored. It's amazing how many well-off people provide for their kids and offer them a semblance of care, but aren't really there for them in the way that their kids want them to be.

Or is this just a function of growing up? Do all children, to some degree, feel disappointed by their parents? Perhaps, that's what it means to become an adult. You become one when you realize that your parents aren't perfect; you accept the fact that they have disappointed you in some way, however minuscule and insignificant on the surface, and you forgive them anyway.

"Ellie, I have to tell you something," Brie says. She has a serious look on her face. So, serious in fact, that I think that something might actually be wrong.

"I've been meaning to tell you this for a very long time. But I just didn't know how to come right out and say it."

"Okay," I say. "You can tell me anything."

"I've been thinking that I don't think I want to be identified as a 'she' anymore. I mean, I'm not entirely sure if I want to be called a 'she'."

I nod. I don't really know what she's talking about. I guess she gets that from the expression on my face so she explains.

"I don't know if I want to transition to being a man, but I'm thinking that maybe I do. So...for now...I just want to be a called 'they.'"

"'They?' Instead of 'she'?" I ask.

"Yep."

"But not 'he'?"

"No, not yet. I have been thinking about this for a bit. I definitely don't want the 'it' pronoun, but also don't want to be called 'he.' Not yet. But I don't exactly feel like a 'she' either."

I nod. I don't really understand, but I'm here for her. She's my sister after all.

"Have you told mom yet?" I ask. Out of the two of them, I think she's the one who will most likely have an issue with this whole thing. She's not one to adapt to change easily.

"No," Brie says. "I wanted to run it by my big sister first."

"Well, I'm glad you did. Flattered actually. But you know that telling me isn't exactly the same thing as telling Mom, right? There's no rehearsal for that."

"Yes, I know." Brie hangs her head.

"Maybe tell Mitch."

"No, he'll just go and tell her and then I won't be able to control how it comes out. He's not one for paying attention to details, you know that, right?"

"Unfortunately, I do," I say with a smile.

"So...what about you? What do you think?"

"I don't really know. I mean, I don't really know anything about this, Brie. But to tell you the truth, I'll call you whatever you want to be called. If you don't feel like the pronoun 'she' applies to you anymore, then who am I to say otherwise?"

Tears start to well up in Brie's eyes. I can't remember the last time I've seen her cry. It was probably when our dog, Charlie, died.

"Brie, don't cry. Please. I'm here for you."

"Why do you think I'm crying, Ellie? Because you're here for me."

Tears run down my cheeks as we hold each other tightly. I haven't felt this close to her in...I can't remember how long. Actually, I'm kind of surprised that she came to me with this.

"You know, for a second there, I thought you were going to come out of the closet to me," I say. "Are you...are you into women?"

"I am," Brie says. "But I'm also into men. I'm not sure I'm ready to make a statement definitively one way or another yet."

"I get that."

"What about you? Have you ever been with a girl?" Brie asks.

"I kissed a girl once. In college. At a party. We were both very drunk and people were cheering us on," I say. "Agh, I'm so embarrassed."

Looking back, I'm actually embarrassed by the fact that I did it because of the audience, not because I kissed a girl.

"What about you? Have you ever been with a girl?" I ask.

"Yep. Dated one actually. She just broke up with me."

"Oh, no. How long were you together?"

"A few months. Not long. But we spent every minute together practically, so it feels much more significant."

I nod. "Well, I'm really sorry about the break up. Those are always hell."

Brie and I sit on the couch and gossip the way that sisters do, the way that we have never gossiped in our lives. It's an amazing feeling. Fun and fulfilling.

We talk and talk and never run out of topics. She opens and finishes a bottle of Pinot Grigio while I stick to Coke.

And then, my phone rings. It's Aiden.

"Hey, where are you?" I ask.

"Hi, Ellie," an unfamiliar voice on the other line says. "My name is Officer Paulson. I have to tell you something."

CHAPTER 33 - ELLIE

WHEN I RUSH TO SEE HIM...

T he world starts to spin at an unusually fast pace as I rush to the hospital and to Aiden. All of the flashing lights outside give me a pounding headache. There's a loud buzzing sound that pierces through my skull and doesn't go away until I arrive on 10th Street. We enter through the emergency room entrance and the bright lights and the sterility of the place makes me sick to my stomach. Literally. I rush to the nearest trashcan and throw up.

Somewhere behind me, I hear the woman at the front desk ask Brie if I'm going to be okay. Even though I don't physically laugh, I find this question remarkably funny. Am I alright? I'm in the emergency room waiting to be seen by a doctor. I'm in the emergency room throwing up in the nearest trashcan, unable or unwilling to even have the courtesy to go into the bathroom. No, lady, clearly, I am NOT alright.

Brie finds out the number and location of Aiden's room and we head there. Only problem is that he's not in the room. No, he's still in surgery and we have to wait in the smaller waiting room in the east wing until he is wheeled into his room.

"He's going to be okay, right? Right?" I keep asking Brie as I pace around the waiting room.

"Yes, of course, he is. Of course," Brie lies through her teeth. She has no way of knowing if he will actually be all right, but I appreciate the gesture. I need something to believe in right about now.

Twenty minutes pass and it feels like it has been an hour. Another ten pass and it feels like it has been three hours.

"I need to do something," I say. "I need to get out of here."

"What? Where are you going to go?"

"I don't know. Where's the nearest vending machine?" I ask. "Or the farthest one? I could use a stroll."

Just then a police officer approaches us. He's dressed in his navy blues and looks very official. Almost like a cop from TV. He introduces himself as Officer Paulson.

"What happened here?" I ask. "What's going on?"

"Did no one tell you?"

I shake my head no.

"Please tell me. I'm Aiden's fiancée."

Officer Paulson looks down at his notebook, trying to avoid my gaze. This must not be his favorite part of the job.

"Mr. Black...Aiden...has been shot," Officer Paulson says, choosing his words very carefully.

"Shot!? Why? By whom?"

Now this is definitely not something that I ever expected in a million years.

"Like mugged?" Brie asks. Yes, of course. A mugging

is definitely a possibility. This is New York after all, a place almost as famous for its muggings as it is for its pizza.

"No, we don't think so," he says.

"What then?"

"Can you tell me what happened? Where he was going?" Officer Paulson asks.

I stare at him. I don't know what he means or why he's asking me these questions.

"He was visiting me beforehand," I say. "I'm pregnant. We're having a baby."

"Oh, okay." By the expression on his face, I can tell that this is news to him.

"Didn't Aiden tell you?"

Officer Paulson ignores this question. "So, you said that he was with you at your apartment? Where was he going, ma'am?"

"I was sick, throwing up. I wanted a bagel. I thought that it would make me feel better. So, he went to the bagel shop at the corner. Is that where this happened?"

Officer Paulson writes something in his little notepad and then looks up at me.

"I have to tell you something, ma'am."

I hate how he calls me ma'am. There's a cold, detached quality to it. It's like he's referring to someone he doesn't really want to go talk to. Even though I want to shake him to knock the words right out of him, I take a step forward and wait patiently for whatever he's about to say.

Why isn't he saying anything? Wait a second. He has been shot. But not seriously, right? The thought of him being actually injured, like seriously injured, didn't actually occur to me until this very moment. Stuff like this doesn't happen to real people. It just happens to people on television, right?

"Aiden has been shot, but he's all right. He's in a coma."

My mind starts to buzz. A throbbing headache forms in the back of my head.

"A coma! No one who is all right is in a coma!"

Why hadn't he told me this originally?

"Ma'am, please calm down. He's going to be okay."

"How can you know this? You can't possibly know this. I need to see a doctor."

At that moment, everything goes to black. People come up and talk to me, saying words that I don't really understand. Luckily, Brie is there to listen and say things in return. I just stand here, waiting until they let me in to see him. A doctor comes out and talks to us in a hushed tone. He uses a lot of medical jargon to explain that Aiden has been shot and they had to put him in a medically-induced coma.

"When will he come out of it?" I ask.

"We're not really sure. We are going to be monitoring him around the clock. I will also be conferring with other doctors in order to make that decision."

That can't be good. You never want your doctor to meet with another doctor or doctors to make a medical decision. That means that something serious is going on, doesn't it?

After a while, the doctor leaves. He answers most of Brie's questions, who, at this moment, is much more levelheaded than I am. Basically, the conclusion is that there's nothing really to do. The situation is what it is and now it's just time to play the waiting and praying game.

After the doctor leaves, Officer Paulson comes over again and introduces me to his colleague, Detective Bradley. Bradley being his last name. Detective? Why is a detective here?

Detective Bradley asks me to repeat my story about what happened. Where was Aiden before he was shot? Why was he going there? I tell him exactly the same thing that I told Officer Paulson. Why the hell is all of this so important anyway, I wonder. I mean, he was going to buy some bagels. What's the big mystery here?

"Detective Bradley, is it?" Brie asks. "Who do you think shot Aiden?"

He takes a step back and looks at Officer Paulson. Now, not only are the doctors conferring about this case, but so are the cops. What the fuck is going on?

"Well, we have a witness. The person who ran over to help Aiden and called 911."

"And?" I ask. "What did they say?"

"He said that Aiden was having trouble talking. But when he asked him what happened, he said one name. And repeated it over and over."

"Whose name?"

"I'm really not supposed to tell you," he says.

"But you're going to, right?" Brie asks.

Detective Bradley looks down at the floor and shuffles his feet. "Okay, but you didn't hear it from me."

We wait.

"Blake Garrison."

CHAPTER 34 - ELLIE

The name Blake Garrison rings through my ears. The cop goes on to explain what the witness saw, but it all goes in one ear and out the other. I ask Brie to repeat it all to me.

"Blake shot him. From what the witness reported, he came up to him, they argued, and just as Aiden was walking away, he shot him," Brie says after the cop leaves us alone.

I feel my blood starting to boil.

"How could he do this? Why? I mean, I knew that he was a piece of shit, but this? What the hell?"

"People do crazy things when they get fired. Or embarrassed. Especially men."

I told Brie the story of what happened. The broad strokes anyway. She's right. Of course, she's right.

The cop and the detective come back and insist that I give them a statement. He wants to know more about Blake and Aiden's history and what could've caused him to do this. Motive. Well, I've got plenty to offer in that department. He takes me aside and I give him the full story. I don't leave anything out. There's no point. Who would I want to protect? Definitely not Blake. No, the truth about who he is and what he's capable of needs to come out once and for all.

"So, where is he now?" I ask.

"We have an ABP out on him," Officer Paulson says. "I'm sure that they will pick him up anytime now."

WE SPEND the rest of the day in the hospital. I throw up every few hours and fall asleep in the waiting room, but I refuse to leave. I can't. I ask Brie to bring me my pills and some comfortable clothes, but they don't do much to make things better. Still, I wait.

Finally, they let us in to see him. I see him lying in the bed with his eyes closed. Lifeless. His skin is pale and splotchy. His hair is dull. He has none of the spark that I have fallen in love with. It's not that he even looks helpless. He just doesn't look like Aiden. Not my Aiden.

No, no, no. This can't be happening. Tears start to run down my face. Please, please, come back, I whisper. I take his hand. It's cold to the touch. He doesn't respond. There's just the steady beeping sound of the machine reminding me that he is still there. Somewhere.

"How long do you want to stay?" Brie asks. I turn around and look at her as if she's insane.

"Forever," I say quickly. "Until he gets better."

"I don't think you can."

"I don't care."

If I can't, then I will deal with this later. But for now, I'm here. And I'm staying here for good.

Minutes turn into hours and I'm still here. I sit next to his bed staring at his face and wondering how it all went so wrong. Brie stays with me even though I ask her not to. There's no need for both of us to lose sleep. Besides, she hardly knows him. But Brie stays anyway. She buries her head in her phone and pretends to work. Apparently, she's working on some article. I can't remember about what.

After a while I can't stand the wait any longer. I need a distraction. I take out my laptop, which Brie was kind enough to bring over along with some clothes and other sundries, and I check my emails. I have a number from my readers and they put a smile on my face. They're asking when the next book in the series is coming out and tell me that they can't wait to read it. In all the badness that surrounds me, these emails give me a glint of hope.

As the hospital quiets down for the night, I prop up my feet on the chair next to me and open the latest Auction book. I have it all outlined, but have a few chapters written. But I couldn't work on it when I was throwing up all the time. I flip to the thriller which I started, but that doesn't seem right now either. I'm no longer in the mood to murder any characters to make myself feel better. No, I miss thinking about love and beauty and all the things that inspired the first book. I miss hope.

I read over the outline of the next chapter and start typing. My head hurts and my eyes are barely staying open and yet I continue to type. The characters get into a big fight and take some time apart. During that time, she reminisces about the all the good times that they've had. Her good times are my good times. A few times, my throat closes up remembering all the laughs that Aiden and I had.

It's going to happen again, I say to myself glancing over at him.

"Just wake up, honey, and I will be here for you. No matter what."

Wow.

Now, there's a statement. I mean, I've said that to him before, I'm sure. We all do in relationships. But do we really mean it? Do we really think that sometime in the future we might be faced with the prospect of really being there for this person? What if he's totally helpless and dysfunctional? What if he can't remember anything? What if he's lost? What if he can't take care of himself physically at all?

Would I be here for him? Can I be here for him?

I don't really know what this means, but I know I want to. I just need him back. No matter what the condition. Back to normal would be best, of course. But I'll take him in any way.

But is that me just being naive? I mean, I have no idea what it's like to have a sick boyfriend to take care of. And I know that I am not the most giving person in the world. I'm quite selfish and self-centered and I don't really know if I can or will change that. Frankly, I don't even know if I'm capable of changing this.

For instance, I like my alone time. A lot. I like to have time to read and think. I like to have time to write and just be by myself. Not many people understand that. My mom never did. But Aiden did. And now what? What's going to happen now? If he's seriously injured? If he has crippling back pain? If he is in a wheelchair? What then? How will I be able to take care of him? I don't really know. But I will try. There's one thing I know for sure, I will do my best. I just hope that will be enough.

By the following morning, Aiden's shooting is all over the news. Reporters are waiting outside the hospital and some are even crawling around the waiting rooms, pretending to be regular visitors. I don't really have the energy to deal with them. Nor do I really know how to deal with them. Should I tell them to leave? Will that just make it worse? Maybe I should just ignore them. They won't go away, but they won't have much of a story to publish.

I chose the latter. The decision isn't exactly incorrect, but it doesn't really solve my problem. They take pictures of me, unflattering at that, and within the hour I see myself on the cover of three online gossip magazines. Perfect. Perhaps, next time I should grant an interview and pose for the photo so I don't look so pathetic and the headline doesn't read 'Aiden Black's Girlfriend Waits for Him to Come Out of the Coma.'

In the morning, Brie comes back with some coffee and pastries from Starbucks. I ask if she's heard anything about Blake and she says that they're still looking for him. She talked to Officer Paulson on the phone before she came over and he didn't really have any news for her.

"So much for that All Points Bulletin, right?" I say.

"They're doing their best," Brie says.

"Yes, I know they are," I say. "I don't know why I said that."

"Because you're tired and pissed off that your fiancé and the father of your unborn child is lying here in a coma while the guy who did this to him is out there running around free."

I stare at her. "Yes, thank you very much, Brie Willoughby, for that detailed explanation and examination of my feelings."

She flashes me a sarcastic smile. I'm about to respond with something witty when a wave of nausea comes over me. I run to the toilet, which is luckily inside the room, and throw up. After I vomit my guts out for a few minutes, my body gets the chills. More like the chills followed by intense heat. I lie down on my side on the cool floor not caring how gross it is to put my face down on the hospital floor and wrap my hands around my knees. A few minutes later, Brie comes in and helps me into the ensuite shower. I let the warm water run down my body and I feel a little bit better. But the sensation doesn't last. I get too hot and throw up again, this time in the shower.

"Fuck," I moan when I get out of the shower, wrapping my towel around me. Brie hands me the bottle of Diclegis pills, which seem to be doing fuck all right now.

"This really sucks," Brie says. "I'm so, so sorry."

I shrug and start to put my clothes back on. Just then there's a knock at the door. The doctor I met last night, and whose name I cannot remember, comes in with a few other people. Dr. Reycook introduces herself again and introduces the residents who are there to learn from Aiden's case. I shake their hands with my hair dripping water on the floor.

She reads over his chart and confers with the others in their white lab coats. Then she turns to me and says, "Everything seems to be okay."

"What does that mean?" I ask.

"Well, we will continue monitoring him, but if he continues to improve, we will take him out of the coma in a few days."

"He's improving?" I ask, looking over at Aiden's almost lifeless body.

"I know that it's difficult to tell, but he is. His heartbeat is stronger and other vital signs are looking good, too."

I ask her more questions, but her answers are not much clearer than that. What is a relief is that he's apparently getting better. When they leave, I walk over to Aiden and take his hand.

"You're going to be fine, honey," I say through the tears. Happy tears. "You see. You're going to be all fine."

Brie stays with me for a while and we spend an hour watching Judge Judy without saying a word. Then, suddenly, something occurs to me.

"Oh, crap, I just remembered. I have my ultrasound appointment today. Fuck, fuck, fuck."

"When?" Brie asks.

"This afternoon. But I guess I can cancel it."

"No, don't. It will take you away from here for a bit. Might be nice. Plus, you need to get the ultrasound sometime anyway, right?"

I shrug. I guess.

"Well, perhaps today is as good a time as any."

DR. EMILY BODON'S office is mysteriously located in a suite with three proctologists. I write my name on the clipboard by the nurses' station and they hand me another clipboard with three pages of questions to answer. Perfect, I think to myself. But I guess it's something to do while I wait. I fill out the info on the clipboard. It doesn't take long. I don't have any diseases and am not taking any medication. I just mark NO all the way down on one long box of questions. When I turn it in, the man at the front desk points out how quickly I managed to fill out the page.

Then I sit and wait. And wait some more. A couple of women come in and are quickly taken back. I ask why they went ahead of me in the nicest way possible. I don't want to be rude since I'm a firm believer that you get more flies with honey than you do with vinegar.

"They are here to see someone else," the front desk guy says. I nod as if I understand, but I suspect that that's a lie. Still, there isn't much I can do about any of it.

A few minutes later, a nurse with a friendly look on her face and a clipboard in one hand calls my name. First, we stop by the scale. Shit. I can barely look. I've gotten so fat. It has only been a few weeks, but I've already gained so much weight. At this rate, I'm going to weigh close to two hundred pounds by the time I give birth.

"I'm getting big?" I say. It's partly a question and

partly a statement. I feel bad because she is actually considerably bigger than I am but I can't help how crappy I feel about how I look.

"No, not at all." She smiles. "I've had three kids."

I guess her statement is supposed to make me feel better, but it doesn't. I just feel worse. And more unattractive. I follow her to the room and she tells me to sit down and that the doctor will be with me soon. I expect to be asked to change into one of those paper gowns, but not this time. Well, that's good I guess. I hate those things.

When she leaves, I look around. There's a big poster of a woman's reproductive organs on the far end next to the magazine rack. I guess it's good that they provide magazines here in addition to the waiting room, but I hate what their presence indicates - that more waiting is involved.

Eventually, Dr. Bodon comes in. She's a small, happy-go-lucky woman in her mid-forties. She asks me how I'm feeling and we talk a little about my vomiting. Now, there's a topic of conversation! She doesn't ask me about the father of the baby and I don't volunteer any information. She wasn't the one who prescribed me the Diclegis; that was a doctor from a different office.

"So, why did you decide to change doctors?" she asks. "Just out of curiosity."

I shrug. I guess I could lie and tell her it was because of all those wonderful reviews I read. That's one of the reasons I had switched, but not the main one. Her office is further away from my house and sort of inconvenient. Plus, the wait here is much longer than it was at the other place.

"Well, I was going to the Advanced Women's Healthcare place before and they have a number of OBGYNs on rotation there. I didn't really like the idea of not knowing who was going to deliver my baby. Plus, they have this policy there of charging you upfront when in reality my insurance is supposed to cover all pre-natal care without any copays."

"And they were trying to charge you for that?" she asks.

I nod. "They were trying to get me to pay for everything upfront and then ask my insurance for a reimbursement. When I called the billing department at my insurance company, they said that they would cover everything and that I couldn't prepay. So, it was getting quite complicated."

She nods.

"So, I knew I needed a new doctor. And you had all these great reviews online," I add. This part is true. I did like all the raving reviews, but this was not the main reason I switched. How perfect is that? Expecting mothers should always select their physicians based on their office's insurance billing practices, right? I mean, it's bad enough that there are some doctors that women just can't go to because they don't accept their insurance, but this? Man, fuck this system.

"Well, I'm glad," Dr. Bodon says. "It took my mom a long time to write them all."

It takes me a moment to realize that she's joking, but when I do, I laugh. A deep loud laugh that comes from somewhere in the pit of my stomach and feels so good that, for a second, I forget about everything else in the world.

"Okay, so do you want to see your baby?" she asks. I nod yes. She turns down the lights and asks me to lie down. I pull up my shirt and she squirts something sticky onto my stomach. She presses the ultrasound wand onto my stomach and looks at the screen. Suddenly, I hear it. The heartbeat.

"Oh, wow. That sounds so fast," I say.

"Yep, babies have a very fast heartbeat," she says and looks back at the screen.

I glance over and see the baby's little head and even smaller body.

"It sounds like it's under water or something," I say.

"Well, it pretty much is," she says.

After moving the wand around my stomach a bit, she looks over at me. "Everything looks good. Judging from the date of your last period, you are seven weeks along."

I nod. Wow. My baby is almost two months in utero. That's hard to believe.

"When will I be able to know the gender?"

"If you want to find out the sex, we can probably tell you around fifteen weeks, but it's not super accurate. Closer to twenty weeks."

"Okay, well, that will give me some time to decide if we even want to know."

Dr. Bodon gives me a smile and then prints out a couple of pictures from the ultrasound. These are mine to keep. I stare at them as I wait to checkout. This is my baby. My baby. Our baby. Mine and Aiden's. That's still so hard to believe. My heart skips a beat. You have to get better, Aiden. You just have to. You have to see your baby.

I nstead of going straight back to the hospital, I decide to stop by my apartment and get a few things. A notebook to write in, a copy of *The Outlander*, a book I've been reading on and off for some time now and my iPad. I need the iPad in case I want to watch some Netflix on something other than my phone or my laptop - the phone is too small and the laptop is too unwieldy.

When I get into the lobby, I get an uneasy feeling down in the pit of my stomach. Agh, I have to take another Diclegis pill. It's wearing off. I fish around for my keys and walk inside. I head straight to the kitchen to wash down the pill with a glass of water.

"Hello, Ellie." A cold, familiar voice sends shivers

down my spine. I know who it is without even turning around.

"Are you surprised to see me?" he asks. My shoulders scrunch up all on their own and a thick mass of tension settles just below my neck.

"What are you doing here, Blake?"

THANK you for reading BLACK CONTRACT!

Can't wait to find out what happens next to Ellie and Aiden and how their story ends? **One-click BLACK LIMIT now!**

Is this the end of us?

I found a woman I can't live without.

We've been through so much. We've had our set backs. But our love is stronger than ever.

We are survivors.

But when they take her from me at the altar, right before she is to become my wife, everything breaks.

I will do anything to free her. **I will do anything to make her mine for good.**

But is that enough? And what if it's not?

One-click BLACK LIMIT Now!

SIGN UP for my **newsletter** to find out when I have new books!

You can also join my Facebook group, **Charlotte Byrd's Steamy Reads**, for exclusive giveaways and sneak peaks of future books.

I appreciate you sharing my books and telling your friends about them. Reviews help readers find my books! Please leave a review on your favorite site.

OTHER BOOKS BY CHARLOTTE BYRD

Debt series (can be read in any order)

DEBT

OFFER

UNKNOWN

WEALTH

ABOUT CHARLOTTE BYRD

Charlotte Byrd is the bestselling author of many contemporary romance novels. She lives in Southern California with her husband, son, and a crazy toy Australian Shepherd. She loves books, hot weather and crystal blue waters.

Write her here:

charlotte@charlotte-byrd.com

Check out her books here:

www.charlotte-byrd.com

Connect with her here:

www.facebook.com/charlottebyrdbooks

Instagram: @charlottebyrdbooks

Twitter: @ByrdAuthor

Facebook Group: Charlotte Byrd's Steamy Reads

Newsletter

COPYRIGHT

Printed in Great Britain
by Amazon